A THIEF IN THE NUDE

OLIVIA WAITE

To all women artists,
but especially to those
whose names we have forgotten.
You are remembered here.

CHAPTER 1

$\mathcal{T}$he first thing went wrong before she even got in the door.

Hecuba Jones had learned to pick locks on the doors of her family's home. Her father had eventually installed a Barron double acting, to challenge her, and it had taken months for Hecuba to find the right amount of pressure to use on the pick—too little and the lock stayed locked, too much and it relocked itself. It had been nearly ten years since she'd tried something that complicated.

The Earl of Underwood was apparently quite mindful of his security, since the lock on the tradesman's entrance to his home was the very latest model: a Chubb detector lock.

Which was, as everyone knew, unpickable. By anyone, much less an amateur thief a full decade out of practice.

She raised the pick and hook to the edge of the lock and took a deep breath, willing her hands to remain steady. The Chubb's main feature was that it could only be unlocked by one specific key. Using a copy—or lifting one of its inner levers the slightest bit too high with a pick—would jam the lock entirely. Then, when the owner came home with the right key, the lock would only open if the key was turned the opposite way—so the lock's owner would know that someone had attempted an entry.

Hecuba's palms grew damp and she scrubbed them against the material of her black trousers. There was no *time* for this, damn it all.

She gritted her teeth and leaned closer.

And paused.

A thought occurred.

She transferred pick and hook to her left hand and reached out with her right. Slowly she wrapped her hand around the door handle and turned it.

The door opened with demure, well-oiled silence.

Hecuba didn't know whether to curse or sing with joy. Instead of doing either, she moved quickly across the threshold and pulled the door quietly shut behind her.

It was a strange thing indeed to move through the darkness of an unfamiliar house. She paused for a long while, just listening, until she was finally convinced that even the most disciplined and devoted servants had long ago sought their beds. Her baggy men's trousers and high-collared coat were deep black and well-worn enough not to rustle or catch the light as she padded along the corridor of the first story. Five minutes and two wrong doors later brought her to the Earl of Underwood's study.

Twin shafts of moonlight slipped in through the two tall and imperfectly curtained windows in the far wall. On the right, a pair of paintings hung above a broad old desk bristling with scars. Two more paintings flanked an ancient, cracked mantelpiece on the room's left-hand side. A few weathered armchairs stood about the room like battered veterans of some ancient upholstery war. One would have expected the earl to be more particular about the state of his décor, but the room was undeniably cozy, in an old-fashioned, masculine kind of way.

She reminded herself not to relax. Despite the room's welcoming air, disaster would result if she were caught here.

Hecuba stepped forward in her soft leather shoes and raised

the darkened lantern. The flick of a wrist set free one slender beam of light, just bright enough for her to see a few telltale colors of the room's four paintings.

Relief bubbled up in her heart. Yes, these were the ones she'd come for.

She set the lantern on the desk and took down the left-hand painting from that wall, handling its carven frame with great care. Night obscured most of the painting's details, but she knew it as well as she knew her own face, and her memory filled in the gaps. This painting showed a twilight scene in the back garden of a country cottage: serenely drooping blossoms, rustic white walls, the merest hint of a dusky blue horizon in the distance. On the balcony of the second story, a tall figure dressed all in black with a black mask over his face pressed his back against that white wall, focused on the tempting open window to his right.

It was titled *The Thief.*

And there was the signature in the lower right-hand corner: *C. F. Jones.*

The painting had caused a scandal and a sensation when it had been offered for auction after the artist's demise. Rumor had it that the masked figure depicted was the culprit behind several highly talked-over burglaries of the previous generation, and that the artist had received payment for his work in the form of priceless, purloined jewels.

Nobody knew *The Thief's* true identity.

Nobody, that is, except Hecuba Jones.

Hecuba turned the painting facedown and snicked open the blade of her knife.

From behind her, a large hand moved into view on her left and snapped the lantern shut.

Hecuba was plunged into darkness.

While she stood frozen in shock, her right hand—with the knife still clutched in it— was pressed gently yet firmly to the rough wood of the desk. A man spoke, so close that his breath stirred the hair by her right ear. "It seems we both have found ourselves a thief," he murmured.

In the dark, with her eyesight not yet readjusted to the moonlight, Hecuba struggled to form a picture of her opponent. Tall, certainly, and neither very old nor very young. The grip of his hand was firm but not painful, and it took a certain confidence to sneak up on a thief in one's own home.

Dear God, he wasn't the earl, was he?

Hecuba's palms grew damp and her mind began to race. Her pulse sped up to match. "Congratulations," she said, with a calmness she only pretended to own. "You've caught me. What do you plan to do now?"

Amusement laced his voice. "It seems an appropriate time to summon the authorities, wouldn't you agree?"

"No, I would not." Hecuba's second knife was in her other hand now. She pressed the point of it against whichever part of his anatomy was behind her and slightly to the left. He sucked in a startled breath. "In fact," she went on, "if you don't release me, I'm going to have to take drastic measures."

There was a thoughtful pause. "Oh, my dear, you are already in enough trouble without staining your hands with the blood of a peer."

She felt him shift and knew he was reaching for the lantern. She pressed the knife slightly more insistently against his body and ordered, "Don't."

He chuckled against her ear. His breath was warm, his laugh was low, and Hecuba cursed silently. Damn it, she should not be getting aroused by the smoky, brandy-laden voice of a man she'd never seen and whose paintings she was here to steal. She could have sworn he'd moved closer, the breadth of his chest a mere inch away from her back. The hair on the back of her neck lifted in awareness. His hand curled more firmly around her wrist and she definitely shouldn't have enjoyed that either. She gripped the knife in her left hand more firmly to balance things out.

"I have to wonder," said the man, "what could have induced

you to steal a painting whose financial value doesn't balance out the risk of the endeavor. It's an unusual piece, of course, but forgive me if I doubt that's what brought you here tonight." He smiled. She knew he smiled—she could practically feel the movement of his lips in the dark.

Stall him. Get him talking. Hecuba swallowed against the kick of her heart. "You'll certainly have a hard time convincing the authorities that someone came in here to steal it," she said. "Especially if you don't have a good description of the thief."

His voice grew a shade warmer. "Just under six feet tall, moderately slender, a husky voice and hair the purest shade of red I've ever seen."

Damn! He'd seen enough, then, before he'd shut that lantern. She'd known she ought to wear a wig or a hat or blackened her hair with soot. But she hadn't a wig, soot took forever to wash out, and all the hats she owned were delicate bonnets that would have been much more useful on a visit for afternoon tea—except for the fact that they were all at least three years out of date.

Why was she thinking about hats at a time like this? *Focus, Hecuba,* she told herself. *You're better than this.* All at once she realized her eyes had adjusted to the darkness. Had his?

It was time to act. "You have until the count of three to release me, my lord."

"No earls here, I'm afraid," he replied equably. "You've been apprehended by the younger son, a mere honorable sir."

"That is too bad for you but it doesn't change my intentions in the slightest."

He laughed again and the sound seemed to ripple along every nerve Hecuba possessed. "And to think I had thought tonight was going to be disappointing," he drawled.

"One," Hecuba counted.

The earl's brother went on as though she hadn't spoken. "I come home early, bored with London's usual mode of dissipated entertainment, and discover that tonight the entertainment has come to me."

"Two." Hecuba subtly shifted her weight from one foot to the other.

His breath teased her ear again when he spoke next. "What else might you intend to steal from me?" he whispered. His lips brushed the tender skin of her earlobe.

Hecuba skipped three. She dropped the knife in her left hand and spun around with an elbow cocked and ready. It slammed into his chest and dropped him to the floor, where he curled up and gasped for his lost breath.

Meanwhile Hecuba was busy slashing the painting free of its frame with the knife in her right hand. Quickly she rolled the canvas into a cylinder, the painted side inward and protected. Before her captor could even lift himself from the floor enough to open the lantern, she was out the nearest window and disappearing fast into the London night.

The Heatherton ball was a complete crush. Hecuba was more than happy to fetch refreshments for her cousins, if only to get away from the ballroom for a minute or two.

It was only when she was returning with a glass of sticky lemonade in each hand that she realized they'd had an ulterior motive for sending her away.

For there were the Misses Pym, Anne and Evangeline, dimpling as hard as they could as their host introduced them to two tall and well-dressed gentlemen. There were giggles and the twinkling of eyes. There were compliments and the blushes they provoked. Flirtation was clearly afoot.

Hecuba sighed and hoped at least one of the gentlemen had half a brain, or else the night would be interminable.

Her cousins managed not to look too disappointed at her reappearance. "Oh, there you are Hecuba," said Anne, the taller of the pair. She quickly looked back at the men with a smile. "My lord, may I introduce my cousin, Miss Jones? Hecuba, this is the

Earl of Underwood—and his brother, the Honorable John Rushmore."

Hecuba went white. Would it be too scandalous to throw both glasses of lemonade on the man and bolt for the door?

But her cousins were already taking their drinks from her and Hecuba could do nothing but sink into a slow curtsey with her head bowed. "My lords," she murmured.

"A pleasure, Miss Jones," said the earl—but Hecuba's attention was fixed on the other man.

John Rushmore was as tall as she'd thought, with brown hair and eyes. Every line of him was strong and angular, though he didn't look nearly as stern as his brother. He looked...clean, streamlined, as though everything unnecessary had been left out or cut away. This was the man who'd stood behind her in the dark one night ago, smelling of brandy and spice, whispering threats into her ear while his hand clasped her wrist at the point where her pulse throbbed.

And he was grinning shamelessly at her.

Dear God, he'd recognized her.

"Miss Jones," he said, bowing over her hand. His satisfied tone could have been mistaken for romantic interest, but Hecuba knew better and she very nearly jerked her arm back out of his grasp. Unfortunately they were in view of a hundred interested people—and her cousins were watching quite closely, along with the earl—so she merely held still while he kissed her hand. She could feel the pressure of his lips on her skin and his fingers on her palm even after he released her. "A pleasure, Miss Jones," Mr. Rushmore said.

He was enjoying her discomfiture. Hecuba's shock sharpened into irritation now that it had a mark. "A platitude, Mr. Rushmore," she replied.

"You're quite right." Hecuba regarded this affability with suspicion, but his face was perfectly bland. "We have barely exchanged names, after all. We cannot possibly know anything about each other."

7

"Nothing, in fact," Hecuba agreed.

Mr. Rushmore leaned forward, his smile turning crooked and challenging. "But of course, there is a pleasure in mystery, isn't there?"

"That pleasure vanishes when the mystery is solved." Hecuba gave him the most brilliant false smile she could muster. "Therefore, sir, in the interest of furthering your pleasure, you may not want to further your acquaintance with me."

Anne blanched while Evangeline glanced from Hecuba to her sister in confusion. The earl blinked and looked suddenly much more wakeful.

The Honorable John Rushmore merely laughed...and there was no reason that sound should warm her or make her heart flutter. It did both, to Hecuba's silent fury.

Anne stepped forward and put her hand on her cousin's arm before she could say anything else. "Hecuba is a little unused to society, Mr. Rushmore," she said. "She has lived most of her life in the country, with parents who were rather, well...eccentric."

Hecuba had long since stopped being surprised when Anne threw these little social daggers her way. In truth, she mostly encouraged it—she had no desire to prance around before a passel of bluebloods who would analyze her hips and her teeth as though those parts of her body foretold what kind of mother she would prove to be. She had no great desire for a wedding or a husband, as Anne did. She also knew that her common background and vivid, unfashionable hair were often considered flaws by the type of gentlemen Anne tried so hard to attract.

But just this once, she wished her cousin thought of her as an ally rather than as competition. As always, when she felt the cold hand of despair, she put her chin up and straightened her spine. "If the gentlemen will pardon me, I feel the need to fetch my own glass of lemonade. It is dreadfully warm in here." She felt Anne's relief like a weight pressing her down as she curtsied to the earl—who looked vaguely disappointed—then turned on her heel and strode away.

She retreated to the gallery, a long, dark space high above the ballroom where she could spy unseen on the colorful spinning of the dancers below. Thick pillars and rounded porticoes allowed a clear view down while the watcher herself remained shielded from sight. Up here, it was easier to discern the patterns and movements of the crowd as a whole: the dancers, of course, had their rhythm and symmetry, but even the movements of the groups in conversation on the fringes were more easily understood from this height. She could see who was being avoided, who was currently the room's center of attention, who was slipping out to the moonlit gardens and who was following after a too-brief period of time. All of society's unspoken rules were so visible when one stood outside them.

All while she remained safe and unseen, wrapped in darkness and solitude.

A voice broke into her thoughts. "I'd hoped not to find you here."

"Then you shouldn't have looked." Hecuba didn't need to turn around to know whose voice had interrupted her. But it felt cowardly to keep her back turned to him— and worse, it felt dangerous, too close to the memory of him behind her the other night.

So she turned around and gave him her coldest expression.

His grin widened and he took his eyes from her to glance at the canvas ancestors that hung on the walls around them. "I must confess to being jealous," he said in that brandy-rich voice of his. "I'd thought you were interested in my paintings and mine alone. But to catch you studying another man's gallery..."

Hecuba gritted her teeth. "I'm not here to steal Lord Heatherton's family portraits," she ground out.

"So there really is something special about my paintings?" Rushmore said immediately. There was a calculating gleam in his eye that suggested his flirtatious tone hid something harder.

Hecuba took a deep breath and wrestled down her irritation.

She would not be drawn into these aristocratic games. "Is there something in particular you want from me, Mr. Rushmore?"

He tilted his head and considered her for a moment. She felt his scrutiny like the press of heat on a scorching summer day, everywhere and nowhere at once. Then he held out a hand. "I would like a dance."

Hecuba folded her arms across her chest. "I am terribly fatigued, sir," she said, happy there was nobody around to hear. "I would make a terrible partner."

His mouth curved in a grin so cunning it made Hecuba suck in a breath and go hot all over. "Would you rather I find our host and inform him that I found you up here, only one night after you successfully stole a painting from my brother's home?"

She stared. "Are you really blackmailing me into dancing with you?"

He took a step forward, hand still out and waiting for hers. "Yes," he said. "Please."

She knew it wasn't really a request and that *please* shouldn't have mattered. But he had her neatly trapped and she still didn't know why he hadn't turned her in yet as the thief she was. She certainly wouldn't find out by avoiding him.

He wasn't smiling anymore.

She glanced at his hand and remembered what it had felt like when he'd held her wrist. Then she mustered up all her reserve and resolve. Surely one simple dance would not destroy her. They would hardly touch at all.

The musicians below launched into a waltz. Obviously the gods were out for blood.

She blew out a breath in vexation and took his hand.

His other hand went to her waist and he pulled her toward him, just slightly closer than propriety recommended. Her treacherous blood raced in her veins and she fought for calm. It was simple anger, she told herself—but even she didn't quite believe it.

The gallery was too small for the sweeping range of motion

enjoyed by the waltzing couples down below, but it didn't matter. Held so close, with his grip so firm on her waist and his hand warm around hers, Hecuba could feel every motion, every tiny step, every gentle sway as they spun slowly in tandem. The slight trembling of her hand in his felt like an earthquake, and every light press of his fingers just above the curve of her hip went through her like a thunderbolt. He began pulling her closer in tiny increments, diminishing the space between them as the circle grew slower and slower until she was very nearly pressed against his chest. His legs tangled in her skirts and made her suddenly very aware of all the layers of fabric that separated them: the silk of her stockings, the cotton of her petticoats, the muslin of her skirts, the fine wool of his trousers. She stopped herself just before she imagined all their clothing away and left them nothing but naked skin.

He bent his head and put his mouth close to her ear. "Steal the second painting tonight," he said.

She couldn't have heard that properly. Maybe the rushing of her own pulse in her ears had gotten in the way of the words he'd actually uttered. "I beg your pardon?" she whispered.

He gazed down into her eyes—and Lord, she could just stretch up one small inch and kiss him if she wanted to. She looked away from him, but she could still feel his eyes on her face and was compelled to look back. As soon as she did, he spoke again. "Come back tonight and steal the second painting. Please."

A mouth that beautiful shouldn't be allowed to form words—especially not the word "please." And she needed that second painting. But he couldn't know that, could he? "And if I say that I have no interest in paintings other than the one I took?"

His lips curved in a smile and really, she mustn't kiss him, mustn't even think of it, even though they were far away with nobody there to see. She could no more banish the thought from her mind than she could banish the air from her lungs. Sooner or later it must surge back in. But he was speaking again. "Then I would call you a liar as well as a thief. They're obviously a set.

You couldn't want one without wanting the others." Hecuba glared daggers up at him but he was unfazed. "Say you'll come."

She wanted to push him away, tell him just what he could do with his precious painting, but—damn him!—he was right. The paintings were indeed a set and she did need all four. "What time?" she asked instead.

For one moment he glowed with eagerness, then that casually flirtatious mask was back in place. "Just past midnight should do it," he said. "My brother is early to bed and early to rise. He'll think nothing of my wanting to stay up late with a bottle in his study ."

"Midnight then," said Hecuba with a sigh of resignation.

He brushed his lips across the plane of her cheek. "You remember the way?"

"It was only last night," Hecuba snapped. "My memory is perfectly in order."

His smile widened and his eyes warmed. "So is mine," he said then his mouth was on hers.

When did we stop dancing? Hecuba wondered in the moment before all thought was obliterated. Then there was nothing but his mouth and his hands pressing her body against the whole length of him. She gasped and he slipped his tongue between her lips, and that was probably wrong but it felt so right that she wrapped her free arm around his shoulders and pulled him toward her for more. He dropped her hand to stroke his palms down the length of her back, all while he coaxed her mouth open wider for him, and his tongue began to tease hers with strokes that surprised her even as they left her breathless.

She had been kissed before, by a long-ago suitor in the first flush of manhood, but that had been a gentle, tentative thing, like a daisy pressed between the pages of a young girl's diary, dried out and delicate. This kiss was a rose. This kiss was wine. This kiss was everything intoxicating and lush and dangerous, precisely the kind of thing an unmarried miss should stay far away from.

Hecuba never wanted it to stop.

But just as she reached for more of the kiss—and for more of the man who was sharing it—he pulled away. Staring into her eyes, he looked just as shaken and startled as Hecuba felt inside. He took a couple of steps back and smoothed the front of his waistcoat. Blushing, she did the same with her skirts. "Tonight then," he said, but there was a note of uncertainty that hadn't been there before.

Hecuba nodded, unsure of her voice. Then Rushmore was gone.

CHAPTER 2

*I*t rained, of course. Hecuba kept her mouth shut but inwardly cursed in two languages—English and a vulgar dialect of French she'd learned from the old cook Father had picked up somewhere during his travels. His cakes had been heavenly but he'd had a mouth like a pigsty. Naturally Hecuba had spent as much time as possible in or near the kitchens, listening in.

More chilling than the rain, though, were the voices she could hear as she crept closer through the darkened grounds around the house. She was approaching from the outside this time, aiming for the long double windows of the earl's study, in case this whole endeavor was a trap set for her by John Rushmore, who was clearly much less honorable than his title implied.

But if there was even a chance she could get away with a second painting...Well, she had to try.

She crouched beneath the windowsill and pressed herself flat against the wall, which kept at least her neck free from the slithery cold of raindrops. She could hear someone—not Rushmore, but perhaps the earl?

"After all your insistence on hanging them together," the voice was saying, "you bring out that old portrait. It's not a painting fit for public viewing, John."

Rushmore's tone was clipped and tight when he responded. "It was an experiment in style, based on Jones' work. I wanted to see how far off I was from a technical standpoint."

The earl laughed. "Probably about as far as Serena threw it when you finally unveiled the thing. I can still see the tear in the canvas where it hit the corner of the mantelpiece."

"I recall," said Rushmore coldly. There was a light clinking of glass and the snap of a log on the fire. Hecuba shivered and wrapped her arms around her torso to hold in as much warmth as she could.

If she were very lucky, she would overhear something useful she could use to blackmail Rushmore the way he had blackmailed her into dancing with him earlier. She spent enough time chafing against the restrictions of genteel propriety with her stern uncle and aunt. She didn't need another person in her life who wanted to control her—particularly an unscrupulous peer who thought only of his own pleasure and how best to achieve it.

The earl was speaking again. "At least it wasn't one of your landscapes. Those gave me nightmares for weeks. I kept dreaming I was in a garden, but it would start to rain and all the paint began to run and the whole world dissolved around me. Terrible." He paused, but there was no response from his sibling. "A good thing you never had to live off the money from your paintings—you'd have starved!"

"At least then the landscapes might have been worth something." Rushmore sounded lively enough, but to Hecuba it sounded like the same thin, tight kind of cheer she put on when Anne made remarks about her eccentric upbringing. Light words that wouldn't chafe the wound beneath. "The artistic world loves nothing more than a dead genius."

It drew a chuckle from the earl. "Well, we all have youthful obsessions we grow out of, I suppose."

"Too bad you never grew out of being an ass."

Hecuba winced—but the earl just laughed harder, his voice moving from one side of the room to the other. "And now I've wounded your pride. I'll let you stew in peace for the rest of the night." A door clicked shut and the conversation was over. Hecuba waited until she heard the clink of glass again then stretched one arm up to tap on the window.

A moment passed before she heard the study window slide open. "Miss Jones?" came Rushmore's voice, barely audible above the steady sound of rain.

"Here," she replied, emerging from beneath the windowsill. He reached out a hand, which felt impossibly warm as it closed around her cold fingers. Pride was cast away in favor of getting out of the cold and the wet and the night. With the leverage Rushmore's hold provided, Hecuba clambered over the sill. Her numb toes were clumsier than usual and she staggered a little upon landing. Rushmore put a hand on her shoulder to steady her even as he clasped his other hand tightly around hers. His jacket was gone, as was his waistcoat, and his shirtsleeves were indecently rolled up nearly to his elbows.

Hecuba looked at his wrists and wondered if her fingers could span them. Carefully she pulled her hand from his.

He gave her a knowing smile and turned to shut the window. Hecuba left him to it and advanced to the hearth and its blazing fire. She put her hands as close to the heat as she could bear, flexing her fingers to restore circulation. Her nose caught the faint aroma of pipe smoke mixed with the scent of old books, while the firelight glinted on the gilt lettering that spelled out the titles and the names of authors. A few candles around the perimeter of the room brightened what corners the firelight didn't reach.

Rushmore poured a quantity of amber liquid into a small tumbler and took it to where she stood shivering by the mantelpiece. "I nearly had an apoplexy thinking you would waltz in while my sainted brother was here."

"I have a bit more sense than that, thank you," Hecuba said.

Rushmore smiled at her again and her heart lurched in her

chest. It was not comfortable and she frowned at him. "A shame," he said. "You waltz beautifully."

"Is that why I'm really here tonight?" she fired back. "Another waltz? Because I am not in the mood, Mr. Rushmore." He grinned more widely still and with an effort Hecuba reined in her irritation. She would never get that second painting by being abrasive, and it was clear Rushmore was going out of his way to provoke her. To give herself a moment to think, Hecuba took a large swallow of what turned out to be whisky. She'd expected brandy and was pleasantly surprised. "This is excellent," she said, but was prevented from elaborating by another bout of the shudders.

Rushmore frowned down at her. "We need to get you out of those clothes."

"*We* need to do no such thing," Hecuba retorted.

"Fine," he said. "*You* need to get out of those clothes, unless you fancy being ill and sore of throat for the next week." She said nothing and he pressed onward. "I'll turn my back, I promise. You can wrap yourself in a blanket, sit by the fire and drink all the whisky you like while your clothes dry."

Hecuba mustered a sharp response, but as she opened her mouth to speak a chill went through her and shook her so hard that she bit down on her tongue. The whisky turned to fire when it struck the tender spot. "Very well," she said instead, "but you will kindly keep your distance."

Rushmore nodded easily, as if sharing drinks with indecently garbed women were part of his everyday experience. Perhaps it was. Hecuba's frown deepened but she accepted the blanket he pulled from one of the armchairs, waited until he'd turned his back, set her whiskey on the mantel, and disrobed with all the speed of which she was capable. Shoes and stockings were spread first on the warm stone hearth, then her black shirt and trousers. Her chemise and drawers were mostly dry, so she kept those on while she retrieved the blanket and wrapped herself in soft green wool. Thankfully she'd left her stays at home; they impeded her range of motion far too much for comfortable burglary.

She turned to find that Rushmore was standing too casually by the window, facing away from her. Firelight danced in the windowpanes.

"You're cheating," said Hecuba, as realization dawned. "I suppose you saw everything in the reflection."

"Not everything," he admitted. "Not nearly as much as I wished."

Hecuba retrieved her whisky and considered hurling it at his head but chose instead to take another swallow. Warmth was beginning to return to her chilled limbs, soaking into her bones with every crackle of flame or sip from the glass in her hand. "You may as well turn around then," she said through the pleasant burn of the liquor.

He turned back toward her and stilled, sweeping her green-draped form with a gaze that went from her damp, tousled hair to the curl of blanket that warmed her bare toes. "Boadicea."

"Bless you," she replied tartly.

He laughed at that. "I'm a painter," he explained. "I see dramatic potential in everything—and you look very much the barbarian warrior queen at present."

Hecuba didn't want to admit how much more pleasing that was than if he'd told her she was beautiful. It warmed her even more than the whisky in her belly or the fire at her back. A change of subject was needed. She looked past him to the wall where *The Thief* had hung before she'd stolen it. Another painting had taken its place.

It was a portrait of a girl in the sunlight. She was laughing at something with her eyes gazing upward and one arm thrown above her head as though to pluck something unseen out of the air. Sunlight—the golden kind you only see at the end of a perfect summer's afternoon—flowed through her chestnut hair and over the graceful curves of her dress, making the bright-red flowers glow behind her. But although all these details were present and remarkably vivid at first glance, the more Hecuba looked at the painting the more they seemed to exist as accidents, ideas created by the merest slash of red or casual sweep of gold. Close up, the individual brushstrokes were plainly distinct, thick bars and bold sweeps of color that her fingers itched to touch.

It was only when she heard Rushmore's voice coming from behind her that she realized she'd dream-walked her way across the entire room and was staring at the painting from one foot away. "That's my sister Serena," Rushmore said.

His sister. Hecuba was first pleased, then angry with herself for being pleased. But she put that aside to stare at the portrait again. "This is like nothing I've ever seen," she said. "You've painted her so vividly she could almost step out of the frame, yet I can see exactly how you've built her out of brushstrokes. It's...it's like when you're just waking up from a dream and you can only half remember what you've been looking at."

He smiled slightly, his own eyes intent on the painting. "My brother objects to seeing it in his study."

"Yes," said Hecuba, "but your brother is an ass."

Rushmore laughed in surprise. "So you heard that part, did you?"

Hecuba's eye was caught by a small irregularity—a part where the painting had been rent then carefully but imperfectly repaired. Phrases from the conversation she'd heard came darting back to the surface of her memory. "This was based on C. F. Jones' technique?"

"It was," he acknowledged. "I was thinking about the way his paintings seem to dissolve at the edges, like they're only half-real, and wanted to see if I could get the whole subject to look that way. I didn't get it quite right, but I think that's partly because the color..." He broke off. Hecuba turned to see him staring at her in rather a more pointed way, those brown eyes of his almost accusing. "Because the color I ought to have used," he said slowly, "was Hecuba green."

"Ah," she murmured. "I'd wondered when you were going to work that part out."

"So that's why you're after my paintings!" he cried. "C. F. Jones was your father."

"No," corrected Hecuba, "C. F. Jones was my *mother.*"

He couldn't have looked more surprised if she'd sprouted an extra head to tell him that fact. "Your mother?" he said. "Are you sure?"

She snorted. "I'm fairly certain, yes."

He stared at her for a moment more then grabbed her by the elbow and hauled her back across the room to the painting that hung to the right of the mantelpiece. Hecuba allowed this liberty because she knew what he was looking for—and because the journey took her back to the warmth of the fire.

In the better light, his eyes flicked back and forth from her face to the face in the second painting, *A Portrait of Hecuba as Henry VIII*, in imitation of the famous Holbein. Hecuba remembered wearing the itchy gold brocade and wrinkled green velvet tunic, the weight of the false crown on her forehead, how much her arms had hurt from holding them at the proper arrogant angle, how her feet had ached to move, how her nose had itched several times and her mother had scolded her for scratching it and spoiling the pose.

She'd stood for two entire days, full of more irritation than an eight-year-old girl should be able to contain. And all that wounded dignity, impatience and fury had been captured in color by her mother's skillful brush, so that eight-year-old Hecuba looked every inch the miniature monarch.

Rushmore apparently saw the resemblance. "Bloody hell," he whispered.

Hecuba saw an opportunity and seized it. "My mother hated wasting time and energy defending her talent on account of her sex, so after she married my father she took his surname as a pseudonym and let all the customers and critics assume she was a man. Of course this meant she couldn't paint portraits without revealing the truth, so all my mother's paintings were landscapes. Except these four. These she painted for herself and for her family. They ought never to have been auctioned off. She meant them to be my inheritance."

He took a deep breath and finally asked the question she'd known he was waiting to ask. "*The Thief?*"

"My father," she said with a sad smile. "He taught me everything I know."

"Bloody hell," he repeated then fell with a thump into a nearby armchair.

CHAPTER 3

John Rushmore glanced from the painting to the woman and back. The blanket she was clutching around her was only a shade away from the impossible green of the tunic in that painting of her as a girl. He'd stared at that portrait for years now, wondering how on earth the artist had gotten that shade of green to stay so vivid when every other artist's green hues went black and dark with age. Hecuba green it was called, and decades later it was still as rich and lustrous as the day C. F. Jones had first raised a hand and put brush to canvas.

And Miss Jones had been there to see it happen.

John was hit by a wave of envy so strong that he had to clench his teeth against the force of it. "Tell me about her," he said, greedy for anything he could learn about the artist he'd idolized for so long. The fact that C. F. Jones was a woman did nothing to change the fact that she was also a genius.

The artist's daughter looked at him in surprise then shrugged and took a seat on a nearby ottoman. In the firelight she appeared mysterious and otherworldly, a Delphic oracle or Pythian priestess come forth to utter strange truths. He waited like a proper supplicant until she began to speak. "Her name was

Cynthia. Her aunt had paid a tutor to teach her watercolors, like any genteel debutante, but my mother convinced him to teach her oils as well. She loved painting people but my grandparents considered female painters shocking and scandalous. They would have cut her off if she painted from life, as other female painters have. Her landscapes became rather fashionable at one point, and sometimes she had to ask my father to act as a go-between with galleries and would-be patrons. They made a game of it, but you could see it hurt her that she couldn't claim her work openly without risking scandal and penury."

The ghost of the little girl she'd been passed briefly over her face. John heard an echo of his brother's laughing voice. *At least it wasn't one of your landscapes.* "I know something about how she must have felt," he said quietly.

She met his eyes then and smiled, her expression warm and open. John took a quick gulp from his glass—the whisky was a less dangerous intoxicant than a smile from Hecuba Jones. He watched a raindrop slide from her hair to her neck, the droplet gleaming like a gem in the firelight. The memory of their kiss slipped through him and left echoes behind, ripples of wind on the surface of a formerly still and untroubled lake. The green blanket had slipped off one shoulder to show the curve of her upper arm and the ivory strap of her chemise. His fingers itched to slide beneath it, to pull it down her arm, to slide both chemise and blanket down and bare the breasts he'd felt against him when he'd waltzed with her in a gallery surrounded by the paintings of other men...

Whereas now she sat in a room surrounded by her mother's most intimate portraits—and they belonged to someone else.

John lurched to his feet and pulled *Henry VIII* from the wall. He walked to the desk, rummaged in a drawer for a knife and sliced the canvas from the frame, just as she'd done the other night. His cravat, once untied, was just long enough to knot around the rolled-up canvas to keep the painting inside safe and hidden from sight.

Then—because he was an artist and couldn't resist a bit of a flourish—he walked back across the study, went to one knee on the floor and with both hands outstretched presented Miss Jones with her own portrait as though it were a victor's trophy.

She took it with one hand, the other holding the blanket closed at her neck. For one brief, blinding second he could see this moment as he would paint it—the shadows of drapery, the warmth of fire on her skin and the halo of light around her brilliant hair. It was all he could do not to drag her up to the north attic where he'd begun a new and secret set of paintings. No one knew about those canvases—not his brother or sister or any of his society friends. They'd so dismissed his earlier work that he couldn't bear to tell them he'd taken it up again, especially when he was still fighting his way through the darkness. Painting had become a slow and painful process, not at all like the brash fire he'd felt when younger, and he was starting to worry that neglect had burned out whatever talent he'd had, like a candle left alone too long in an empty room.

But now he felt all the old urgency return. The vision in his head was clawing its way out through his flesh and every moment spent *not* painting was a moment wasted. He forgot every mocking thing his brother had said, every worry he'd nursed about failure, every ambition he still cherished despite the obstacles. He forgot that he was still down on one knee before a strange woman who'd stolen secretly into the house in the dead of night. The only thing that mattered was this moment. He stared openly, committing to memory each fold of cloth, the angles of her face in firelight, the way her still-damp hair curled close against the luster of her skin, the shadows that threatened her on every side. All of it soaked into him like water in the desert and still it was not enough.

And then, slowly, Miss Jones bent down and pressed her mouth to his.

The kiss blazed through him, soft though it was, and all thoughts of painting fled at the rush of pure physical need. John raised one hand to touch her cheek, to thread his fingers through that lustrous hair...

And his hand bumped the roll of canvas she still held.

The spell was broken and the kiss followed suit. John sat back on his heels while Miss Jones blinked down at him in surprise and, he could see, dismay. But this felt too important to get wrong, and he was getting it wrong.

John surged to his feet and took a few hasty steps back. Her lips were still slightly parted and when she licked them the action was enough nearly to drive him back to his knees. But instead he dredged up all the dusty moral rectitude he had left and said, "I propose a bargain."

She narrowed her eyes. "What kind of bargain?" she asked. He couldn't blame her for being wary. This was all highly improper, and she had no reason to trust him. John only hoped that because he'd kept her secret for nearly a day, she'd be willing to grant him a hearing.

The idea was only half sketched in his mind and he hurried to put words around it. "I'll trade your mother's paintings for the opportunity to paint her daughter's portrait. Your portrait."

Miss Jones widened her eyes but considered it. "All four of Mother's for one painting of yours?"

John took a risk. "A one-to-one exchange. Your mother's paintings for four of mine." He waited on tenterhooks while she considered his offer. He could easily paint a dozen portraits of this woman—a hundred—but that would be highway robbery, thoroughly unscrupulous of him to demand. Besides, she'd never agree to so steep a price.

"A few more trifling questions," she said eventually. John braced himself at the steel in her tone. "Are these for public display or your personal collection? How long will sittings take? Where are they to occur? What kind of garments will I be wearing? Because, Mr. Rushmore, I have no intention of posing in the nude."

She hadn't rejected him entirely. He took heart from that and answered her as best he could. "The portraits will remain secret. I don't know precisely how long each painting will take, but probably no more than one night each—I can always fill in the details on my own. We'll be working in the north attic, where I've set up a studio with plenty of light during the day and plenty of mirrors for reflecting candlelight during evening sessions as well. I assume that late nights and clandestine hours would suit you more than mornings or afternoons?" She nodded and he went on. "I have painted nudes in the past—what artist hasn't?—but that's not what I want from you."

She tilted her head to one side, considering. "What precisely *do* you want from me?" she asked.

He looked at her again, sitting proud and tall in the firelight. "I want the spark," he said bluntly. She remained silent and he felt emboldened to explain further. "Every gesture you make, every unconscious pose you strike, makes me think of a painting. Everything—your voice, your hands, your hair, the way you stand, the way you frown. I've never felt this...this *lit up* before and I'm unwilling to dismiss it or try to ignore it and hope it goes away. I don't want it to go away, though it's not precisely comfortable. I need to capture just a little bit of that on canvas, because if I don't at least try I will regret it for the rest of my life."

"It's not just because I'm my mother's daughter?"

"It's because you're *you*," said John. "I think your mother was a skilled enough painter to recognize a muse when she saw one."

For a long while Miss Jones was silent, merely watching him, clearly trying to gauge the level of his sincerity and her own willingness to go along with what appeared to be the project of a desperate, lonely lunatic. He felt strangely exposed, as though every word had stripped a garment from him and now he stood naked before her. He clenched his hands at his sides to keep his arms from folding defensively across his chest.

Then Miss Hecuba Jones nodded again with an air of finality. "Your bargain is a fair one, I think," she said. "We are agreed."

She set the rolled painting aside and put out her hand to seal the compact.

It was so formal, so businesslike a gesture that John almost laughed. Instead he held out his hand and shook hers.

He didn't want to let go.

He *should* let go. Even though she had agreed to sit for him, she still didn't trust him completely. But her palm was warm and slightly calloused and he was already imagining how it would feel on his bare skin. Desire blazed up again and threatened to burn away what scraps of conscience still remained to him.

John stared down at her, caught between letting her go and letting *himself* go, until her hand tugged impatiently in his. He dropped it at once and retreated until the desk bumped into the back of his upper thighs. He was breathing deeply, as though he'd thought to climb a mountain unprepared and been forced back by the chilly thinness of the air around the peak.

By God, if he could get through a single portrait of Hecuba Jones without throwing himself at her feet and begging her for mercy it would be a miracle.

She brushed her hand idly along the soft nap of the blanket on her knee. He wondered whether she was enjoying the softness against her skin or whether it was a nervous habit she had. "There is something I want to tell you, Mr. Rushmore. Since we have already ventured somewhat beyond the pale."

His brain refused to work. He nodded dumbly.

Her gaze met his again. "I am concerned about my reputation," she confessed, "but not about the actual fact of my virtue." John's breath left him in a rush of surprise. She pressed on. "I have put aside the idea of marriage, quite decisively. I have other plans for my future. Nevertheless there is something appealing in the notion of a discreetly enjoyed affair. So...without going so far as to yield entirely, I must admit that I am somewhat susceptible to your attentions. Improper though they may be."

She was going to kill him, really she was. "I am quite glad to hear that, Miss Jones." If she looked below his waist, she would see precisely *how* glad.

She took a deep breath, the blanket rising and falling. "You mentioned wanting to capture a spark, Mr. Rushmore. For the past two days I've been fighting a spark of a different sort." She reached for her whisky, drained the glass and set it aside. "I'm speaking of attraction, of course. Physical desire." He couldn't look away from her face, which was as serene and composed as if she had this sort of conversation every day. Fire flickered over her lips as they shaped her next words. "This impulse is getting increasingly difficult to ignore, Mr. Rushmore, so I'll ask you quite frankly—what do you plan to do about it?"

John did laugh at that. It was the only thing he could do. "I'd planned to do nothing, Miss Jones," he said, "but it seems I keep losing control and kissing you. For the past few minutes I have been struggling to remember that I am a gentleman." It was shocking to be speaking these words. Flirtations were supposed to be couched in delicate euphemisms, sideways language and subtle allusions. One was never supposed to simply *admit* one was attracted. It was appalling—and more than a little thrilling, as John acknowledged to himself. "But your confession does place this...susceptibility in a new light. So I would ask in return—what should you like me to do about it?"

"Well," she murmured. She smiled at him again and this time her smile was sly. "If it's up to me..."

Miss Jones rose to her feet and dropped the blanket.

Green wool puddled at her feet. John very nearly did the same. Her chemise and drawers were of fine lawn, and the firelight behind her showed him the curves of her figure beneath them.

So much for moral rectitude.

In three steps he was across the room and his mouth claimed hers. Her lips parted and her tongue slid boldly against his, but through the haze of arousal he forced himself to go more slowly than his body demanded. She was still a maiden, after all—a clever, larcenous and frankly sensual one, but a maiden nonetheless.

If he died from this kiss, it would be worth it.

She tasted like whisky warmed by firelight, but when John trailed one hand along her cheek and into the hair at her temple, his fingers grew damp and cool with rainwater. She shivered a little as droplets fell on her shoulder. He couldn't resist the urge to trace his mouth over the skin where those raindrops landed. She shivered again and pulled his mouth back to hers, her own fingers clutching the front of his shirt and sliding into the neck where his absent cravat left him open for exploration. His whole body was hard and ready and trembling from the effort of holding back, so when she scraped one gentle fingernail over the sensitive skin of his chest he gasped in shock and knew he was about to lose the battle against his own desire.

He pulled slightly away and pressed his hands on top of hers, flattening her palms against his chest just over his heart. Her fingertips were beneath the soft linen of his shirt, burning into his awareness, while her eyes sparkled up at him in the flickering light.

"This is a very dangerous thing for us to be doing," he said, his breathing harsh.

She smiled teasingly at him. "Especially now that I know you're just as fearful of this as I am."

"I'm not frightened of you," he said. It was quite possibly the biggest lie he'd ever uttered.

She didn't answer that. Instead she leaned forward, brushing her lips against the backs of his hands. John gasped, then groaned when he felt her tongue lick briefly at the tender skin of his knuckles. "You have such beautiful hands."

"Jesus Christ," he breathed.

She leaned forward again and took the very tip of his middle finger into her mouth.

John froze, all his muscles tense, his cock swollen and hard, all his awareness focused on the finger between her lips. If he let himself move, all would be lost—he would take her down to the carpet and fuck her senseless, self-control and preventative measures be damned. He shouldn't have poured her that whisky —he shouldn't have poured *himself* that whisky...

When she nipped gently at his finger, everything came loose at once.

He surged forward, lifting her from the ground and only stopping when her back met the empty wall where her portrait had once been displayed. He trapped her there with the full weight of his body, glorying in the way she arched against him and in the press of her breasts with only his shirt and her chemise between then. Her arms wrapped around his shoulders and pulled him closer while he ravaged her mouth, teasing and taking and doing his best to torture her as much as she did him. It was rough, desperate, a tempest he couldn't hold back, so he gave in and let his right hand slide from the curve of her waist upward, to capture one breast.

The weight of her against his palm shook him to the core, but before he could do more than savor the feeling she pulled her mouth from his and gasped, "Wait."

And just like that the storm was his to control, though its strength had not lessened. He removed his hand from her breast and put it flat against the wall, where it had a chance of behaving itself. They were both panting, and John pulled away slightly to give her some room to draw breath. Her hands slid from his shoulders and came to rest on his chest again, as though she didn't know whether to pull him close or push him away. She looked more than a bit ravished, hair tousled and lips reddened, and John felt like the worst of cads. Even now he wanted nothing more than another of those mind- destroying, soul-obliterating kisses—but not if it came at the expense of her safety, her comfort or her inclination. "I'm sorry," he said, his gut twisting.

"I'm not," she replied, and just like that John could breathe easier. "I started it, if you recall."

As though he could forget that moment if he lived to be a

thousand years old. "You might have started it but you also called a halt." His brain was still fizzing with desire, so he let go of her waist and put both hands firmly behind his back, clenching them together in case they got him in trouble again.

She shook her head and her fingers curled into the softness of his shirt. "This...this was too much, all at once," she said. "I couldn't keep up."

His hands unclenched at the sadness he heard in her voice. Gently he put his arms around her shoulders, waiting to see if she wanted to pull away. Instead she sighed and leaned into him, so he allowed himself to relax into the embrace and rest his cheek on the top of her head. "You don't have to keep up," he said. "Wherever this takes us, we go together."

They stayed that way, simply holding each other, while their breathing settled into a regular pattern and even their pulses kept matching time. It was the single most intimate moment John could remember having with another human being. He tried to imagine painting it, trying to fix on canvas the sense of warmth, of something newborn and fragile just coming into the world—but no palette, no subject seemed enough to contain it. For the first time his imagination failed him: all he could do was feel.

Eventually, however, time intruded as a clock chimed the hour —one o' clock. "It's late," he said.

"I should be getting back," Hecuba agreed at once. "Do you mind watching over *Henry VIII* a little longer? I shouldn't risk it in the rain."

"Of course." John hesitated. "Do you need me to arrange a way for you to get home?" he asked. "I could..."

She waved away his concern. "It's merely a few minutes' walk, through the richest neighborhood in London. And I know the shadows—I can manage easily, even in this weather."

On how many nights had she stolen alone through the darkened city? A mixture of distress and admiration poured uneasily through him, the two emotions inseparable. John stood apart, considering this, and watched as she donned her now-dry clothing and became a thief once again. Standing there in those black trousers, as mischief lit her eyes...

She caught him looking and quirked an eyebrow at him. "You aren't seriously thinking of painting me dressed like this, are you?" she demanded.

He blinked at being caught out, then grinned. "I'm thinking of doing many things to you dressed like that."

She blushed but couldn't stop the corners of her lips from turning up. "Tomorrow night?"

John would have agreed, but when he opened his mouth to do so it turned into a yawn. "Best make it two nights from now," he said ruefully. "I can't paint properly if I haven't slept well."

She tilted her head in agreement. "Two nights," she said, "for you to recover." In the space of a heartbeat and with another sly smile, she was gone.

John took the rolled-up portrait upstairs with him, thinking that Henry VIII himself had not been nearly as dangerous as Hecuba Jones.

CHAPTER 4

*T*wo nights later, Hecuba crept through the study window again.

The weather was dry, thankfully, but nevertheless Mr. Rushmore offered her a glass of whisky. "My brother's asleep, but we'll still have to be careful." When she nodded, he held out his hand.

She took it and hoped hers wasn't trembling too noticeably.

Their glasses caught what little light there was as he led her down the hallway. A very subtly masked door led to a narrow stairway—a servant's stair, obviously. Rushmore moved with a silence that surprised Hecuba, until she looked down and saw he was in his stocking feet.

She smothered a laugh as they ascended the stairs.

The north attic was three stories up: a cool, high-ceilinged space that overlooked the street on one side and on the other the small garden behind the house. Mr. Rushmore began lighting candles and placing them at strategic points around an open space at one end of the attic.

The sharp scent of turpentine laced the air.

She hadn't realized before that a scent could wrap itself so fully around her memory. Years fell away and she was five years old again in a scratchy brocade dress, or demolishing brightly colored stones in a mortar and pestle the day before her tenth birthday—or the summer she'd turned thirteen and her mother had set her to preparing new canvases while a fading Cynthia Jones put the final touches on her last landscape.

Hecuba swallowed the old grief and looked around, reorienting herself as the light increased. This was not the neat, ordered studio her mother had filled with light and laughter. There was an obsessive, distracted air about the space. Presumably there was furniture in here somewhere, but it lay beneath a sea of paper, paints, gessoed canvases and a tidal froth of pale studies and sketches. Hecuba lifted one loose sheet from a nearby stack and saw a figure captured in hasty charcoal lines, viewed from behind in the process of pulling off a billowy shirt. There was a subtle feminine curve to the hips and in the line of the small of the back, which was the sketch's focal point. That blank space was traced by a spine outlined in a single charcoal stroke, whose boldness and beauty took her breath away. The image was furtive and erotic, unabashedly voyeuristic.

She narrowed her eyes at Mr. Rushmore. "From the other night?" she asked.

He grinned and rolled up the sleeves of his shirt, an old one much muddied by gray and brown smudges—pencil and charcoal and chalk. "I've been like a man possessed," he said, "sketching at all hours, going through reams of paper, always sending out for more supplies. I spent hours this afternoon grinding powders and mixing hues." Candlelight gleamed on his dark hair and the planes of his cheek as he picked up a canvas with a prepared background and placed it on an easel. He gestured to a screen in the attic's far corner. "There's a selection of costumes and draperies and other props behind there. Choose whichever you like."

Hecuba set her whisky to one side and went to investigate.

A riot of color and texture greeted her—most of them false velvets and paste jewels and theater castoffs. But there were masquerade costumes as well and things that were old enough and fine enough that she could identify them as family artifacts. Hecuba trailed her hand over one deep black velvet gown, but hesitated to try on something that had clearly come down through the distinguished Rushmore lineage. What would the ghost of his noble ancestress think to find her sumptuous silks and velvets put to such a use?

Instead she chose an amber gown in an ancient style. Her clothing fell silently to the floor and she was glad not to have to navigate the confinement of stays. Even without them it took her a few awkward moments to pull the garment over her head, and she felt a few locks of hair pull away from the knot at the back of her neck. The dress was slightly too large, so she found a long rope with flaking gilt paint and wrapped it around her waist.

She allowed herself a few deep breaths to try to calm her nerves. It was no use telling herself there was no reason to be nervous, that she'd sat for portraits before. This was different—she felt exposed and raw, as though by letting this man paint her image she was handing over some vital part of herself.

If that was the case, it would be necessary to make certain she gained something from him in return.

She flexed her fingers, took another breath and stepped out into the light.

Mr. Rushmore looked up with a smile on his lips—but almost at once the smile vanished, replaced by a look of such intensity that Hecuba almost retreated back behind the safety of the screen. But he didn't speak, merely stared. Eventually she frowned at him, grabbed the glass of whisky and downed it all in one long gulp.

"Wait," he said, a single syllable humming with urgency. He dragged a chair and small table to the edge of the pool of candlelight, right on the boundary between brightness and shadow. Hecuba sat in the chair as indicated and Mr. Rushmore placed his own glass in front of her. The liquid glowed in the light that spilled over Hecuba's shoulder.

She went still when she felt his hands on her hair.

His fingers were easy and gentle, loosening the knot at her neck and pulling out a few strands to match those she'd dislodged when putting on the gown. Each light touch was a separate star in the darkness, but she simply tightened her hands on the tumbler instead of reaching for him.

He moved back behind his easel and looked at her, considering. Hecuba knew she was slouching slightly and partly shadowed and that her hair must look positively wild. She sent Mr. Rushmore her most dignified glare.

At once, he grinned. "Circe," he said and his hands reached for a brush.

Circe—the ancient sorceress famous for turning men into pigs. A woman who knew the secret road to the underworld and whose singing ensnared the unwary. Yes, that was much better than a nymph or maiden whose only distinction was beauty and whose only role was to be some god's hapless victim. Circe had victims of her own. The thought made Hecuba smile.

The painter's brush paused at the end of a stroke, the artist's eyes narrowing, alight. "Oh, yes—that's..." He trailed off and began to work more feverishly still.

For hours Mr. Rushmore painted, glancing between his model and the canvas while his right arm rose and fell in a broken rhythm. Hecuba tried not to fidget, though nothing in the world made her want to move like being required to keep still.

At least her thoughts could move freely. She watched Mr. Rushmore and allowed herself to imagine what she would do to each individual part of him as soon as the work was finished. She would taste the corner of his mouth and the spot on his lip he bit when he was thinking particularly hard. She would smooth the furrows in his brow then trace her fingers over the yellow smudge on his temple, where he'd absently rubbed a paint-stained hand. She wanted to put her mouth right on his collarbone, which the open neck of his shirt left bare. Then she would pull his hands to her breasts and make him touch her the way he had the other night.

And this time she wouldn't stop.

By the time Mr. Rushmore stepped away from the painting, Hecuba no longer knew whether the stiffness in her limbs and the ache in her joints were from holding still or holding back. She rolled her shoulders as Mr. Rushmore set paints and brushes aside. "It's done," he said. "Or as nearly done as it can be tonight. I'll add the finishing details once this layer has dried." There was a note of sudden shyness to his voice when he asked, "Would you like to see it?"

"Very much." Hecuba rose and walked around the easel, taking the whisky with her. She handed the glass to Mr. Rushmore and he must have taken it—but by then Hecuba had stopped paying attention to anything other than the painting.

She was hunched—and wild, as she'd feared. She was also twined in shadow, limned in light, a hybrid thing of darkness and flame. The whisky had become a brazen goblet, shining in her hands like a miniature sun. She recognized the glare on her face, directed across the room at a bronze mirror—and in that mirror was her face again, smiling in a way that allured nearly as much as it threatened, gazing not at Circe-Hecuba but at Hecuba herself.

It was an old painter's trick, she knew, to put in a reflection that looked back at the viewer. But it made her shiver nonetheless. She leaned in and looked more closely at the brushwork. The layers of paint in the light areas had the effortless precision of long practice, but the brushwork in the shadows...

Hecuba sucked in a breath. All the dark areas of the canvas were populated. A curve here outlined a hunched shoulder, a series of short lines became a reaching, desperate hand. Ghostly limbs and hints of bodies lurked everywhere, visible only in the way certain lines of paint dashed across the canvas. From far away the shadow figures would be unnoticeable—from nearby, they were perfectly eerie. "How on earth did you think to paint the darkness like that?" she breathed.

Rushmore made a strangled sound of surprise when he noticed. "I didn't think," he replied, leaning closer to the canvas. "That was just the way the brush wanted to move."

Hecuba looked at him as he stared in astonishment at his own painting, as if it were someone else's hands that had brought color and line into vivid life with talent and skill. "I suspect you may be a genius, Mr. Rushmore."

He shrugged, his eyes still on her likeness. "I just wish I'd found a brighter gold to work with."

"That's easy enough," Hecuba said, pointing to one particular orange hue. "If you add more ammonia to your Naples yellow, it will temper the hue of the finished paint."

He stared at her in silence.

She lifted her chin, girding herself to be challenged. "I used to help my mother to mix her pigments."

His mouth lifted in a delighted smile. "Even Hecuba green?"

She shook her head. "The color is poisonous and the recipe complex—she never let me near it." Her fingers plucked absently at the rough rope of her belt.

"A pity," he replied. "That was a secret that the world will regret losing."

Hecuba considered telling him that it might not have been lost, not quite, but thought better of it. Three days ago this man had blackmailed her into a waltz and a nighttime rendezvous. They might have achieved a measure of trust since then, but three days was a very short time. There was no need to give away all her secrets just yet.

Especially since the connection she felt to Mr. Rushmore could easily be chalked up to pure, unadulterated lust. Even now candlelight gleamed on his dark hair and slid beguilingly over his skin. She wanted to put her hands everywhere the light touched— then to send her fingers slipping into the shadowed places on him as well. She distrusted this impulse for its power as much as for its impropriety.

He turned and caught her gaze, a half smile hovering on his lips. Suddenly Hecuba knew, with a profound and unsettling certainty, that this man could change her life in ways she couldn't possibly foretell. The course she'd laid out for her own future would be altered and she would careen down another, wilder path. Although for a moment this revelation froze the blood in her veins and the breath in her lungs, in the next instant she rose onto the tips of her toes and kissed him, winding her hands around his neck for balance and trusting that she'd find her feet again when she needed to.

Hecuba Jones had never run away from a challenge. And predictability was much too highly esteemed.

He tasted dark, notes of whisky and smoke and the bitter tang of paint. For a heartbeat he remained stiff with surprise—then his arms curved around her, one hand resting on the small of her back and the other tangling in the hair at the back of her neck while he returned her kiss.

It was all the encouragement she needed. Her heels hit the floor as she loosened her arms from his neck and began to pull his shirt from the waistband of his trousers.

He laughed in shock, but his hands went around hers and stilled them. "What on earth are you doing, Miss Jones?"

"Disrobing you," she said. "Ask me what I plan to do after that."

He groaned, a sound as resonant with need as Hecuba could have hoped. But he still kept her hands pinioned. "I'm not convinced you have thought this through."

"Because I am a virgin I do not know my own mind? Or rather: my own body?" Hecuba scoffed and gave up trying to pull at his shirt. Instead she leaned closer and pressed their joined hands flush against that part of her that ached and throbbed at the juncture of her thighs. "I assure you, Mr. Rushmore, I know *precisely* how and where I need you."

"Oh God." He tipped his head back, eyes screwed shut. Hecuba brushed her lips over his collarbone and felt him gasp beneath her mouth. Then, lightly and deliberately, she flicked her tongue out against his skin.

Mr. Rushmore shook. His hands tightened almost painfully around her wrists. "Wait," he said, a choked sound.

Hecuba lifted her head. She'd asked him to wait two nights earlier and he had. So Hecuba took a deep breath and stepped back, though she kept hold of his hands. His fingers relaxed their grip, allowing her to twine her fingers more closely with his.

At length, his eyes opened and his gaze met hers. "It's not about you," he said. "It's myself I don't trust." He looked away then back while his fingers tightened and released. Hecuba wasn't entirely sure he knew he was doing it. "It's all too much," he blurted out. "The painting, your innocence, your desire, mine...I can't keep it all sorted out in my own mind and I despise myself for the inconsistency." He blew out a long breath. "I've always been able to keep control before, in love affairs. But you...this...it's totally different. I'm worried I'll go too fast or too slow. How can I tell how to proceed when I can barely tell which way is up?"

He was trembling slightly as he spoke. Hecuba wrapped her arms around his waist and leaned in to him. He relaxed slightly as she began to speak. "When I was younger," she said, "I took lessons in the mornings with my cousins and their governess. Reading, mathematics—that sort of thing. The afternoons were for learning deportment and dancing and other such skills, but my parents were too poor and too low in society to care much about making me an accomplished young lady. Once lessons were over, I trailed my father around the house as he taught me how to walk silently, how to pick locks, how to dress to stand out or blend in with the background. Or else I ran wild in the village with the tradesmen's children." She let her polished tones slide back into the flat country accent of her youth as she went on. "There's not a lot of mystery left between men and women when your best friends are the daughters of a barmaid and the village tailor. We guessed most of it fairly early on. We learned the rest as we grew older."

Hecuba pulled back and saw that Mr. Rushmore was looking at her with astonishment but none of the censure she'd feared to see. She put on her gentry voice again, a habit which had become easier and easier over the years. Sometimes she wondered whether she even had what could be considered a natural way of speaking or whether it had all become masks she could put on and take off at will. "The world has a great many rules for those of us who live in it. We learn not to expect the same kind of behavior from a dairymaid as we would from a duchess."

"You'd be surprised," he murmured with a ghost of his former humor.

Hecuba sent him a quelling glance. "I had to learn several different sets of rules growing up, which makes it easier for me to adapt when the world shifts and old habits no longer apply. You had no such advantage. Right now you are troubled because all your rules for how to deal with me have been overturned. I am either too virginal or not virginal enough. You said it yourself— you want either to idolize me or to seduce me. You're failing to do either."

His mouth tightened into a grim line at the frankness of her statement. "Do you have a solution then?"

"Yes," Hecuba replied. "*Listen* to me, Mr. Rushmore. Believe that I want you as badly as you want me. Trust me to tell you what I need, and I will trust you to do the same." She glanced down at their joined hands. "My cousins and my aunt have brought home to me just what I can hope to find in a husband: a steady man, probably a great deal older than myself, who cares more for his own domestic comfort than for anything personally or physically appealing about me. He will have neither title nor fortune and yet he will expect me to be grateful for the opportunity of bearing his children and managing his household. My allowance will be meager if he provides one at all—and should I ever betray by word or deed that I have some dream or thought or desire that does not revolve around him, he will be gravely disappointed." Her gaze lifted again, her mouth set firm. "You'll forgive me when I say that the ruin of my virtue in a blaze of passion is much less dangerous to me than the dull, drawn-out oppression of a life barely lived."

Mr. Rushmore was looking at her very keenly now. Hecuba forced herself to breathe deeply and evenly because holding her breath in suspense was unproductive. She felt lightheaded enough as it was.

Mr. Rushmore nodded once in sharp decision. "A blaze of passion," he said. "I like the sound of that." His eyes on hers were resolved. "But I still insist that we go slowly."

Hecuba felt a ripple of anxiety, which dissolved when Mr. Rushmore leaned down, slid the strap of the Grecian gown to one side and put his lips to her shoulder.

The gentle touch scored through her, a comet blazing across the sky between them. Hecuba held still, afraid that if she moved the spell would be broken. He moved deliberately, leisurely over her skin, spreading fire wherever his lips touched, going as slowly as he'd promised. She fisted her hands in her skirts to keep herself from reaching out to hurry him. It was torture, but she was determined. She would stand firm and let him proceed at his own pace. She would *not* submit, even though he flicked his tongue out to taste the hollow of her collarbone and set her pulse dancing within her. It didn't matter that he leaned close enough that she could smell the spice of him with each shuddering breath. It was nothing to her if all her nerves were alive to the fact that his tall, hard body was separated from hers by the merest few inches of space.

Mr. Rushmore slid the second strap off her shoulder, and the bodice of the amber gown tumbled down around her clenched hands. Hecuba fought back a moan. The gilt rope held the garment around her waist, but her bosom was now naked in the chill attic air.

Though not for long. One of his hands slipped to her waist and the other closed warm and firm around her breast.

Hecuba screwed her eyes shut as the shock of that touch

streaked through her. He moved his lips to her ear. "This isn't *too* slow I hope?" he asked.

The laughter in his voice surprised her into opening her eyes. He was *grinning* at her. She glared at him in return. "You devious bastard..." The words trailed away on a gasp as his fingers pinched her nipple and his teeth closed on the tender lobe of her ear. He chuckled. That dark, lush sound finally undid all her reserve. Her better intentions fell away and took her inhibitions with them.

She unclenched her hands from the fabric and loosened the gilt rope belt. It fell to the floor and took the gown with it, leaving her clad in nothing but candlelight.

She half expected him to pull away, but instead he bore her down to the floor and pushed one trousered thigh between her spread legs. Hecuba had but a moment to glory in the friction of his clothes against her bare skin before he leaned down and took her nipple in his mouth.

Heat and pressure and the sweet, sliding motion of his tongue soon had her writhing beneath him, the floorboards hard and cool against her naked back. His weight pinned her in place, though it was pure delight to arch up and feel the heft of him against all the points on her body that were crying out for more contact. When he lifted his head from her breast, she took advantage of the respite to say, "Your clothes, Mr. Rushmore."

"What of them, Miss Jones?" he returned. Hecuba had no time to muster a reply before he bent and slid further down her body. She jumped a little when he brushed kisses along the sensitive curve of her stomach, the warmth of his mouth a counterpoint to the rough scrape of his jawline.

"Are you going to remove them?" she went on, though words were increasingly difficult to arrange amid the tumult of her senses.

He smiled against her skin. "I'm wearing only a shirt and trousers, Miss Jones."

"Socks," Hecuba pointed out, lifting one leg and sliding the sole of her bare foot along the back of his calf.

"And socks," he agreed on a gratifying moan. He splayed his hands wide on her hips as he slid lower still, holding her fixed and bending down to press his mouth against the throbbing bud between her legs. Hecuba gasped and trembled as he punctuated his next sentence with long licks from that clever tongue. "No boots...no waistcoat...no coat...no gloves...no cravat." He gave her a teasing glance, arch with false dignity. "And you want me to be even less presentably attired?"

She didn't know why he was demurring, but she didn't particularly care. Instead Hecuba groaned, threaded her fingers through his hair and pushed his head back down.

He sighed with pleasure, the sound rumbling through her and adding to the pitch of her arousal. His tongue left no part of her untasted while she arched and cursed and begged for more, pressing her heels against the floor to push herself more firmly against that wonderful, devilish mouth. There came a point when Hecuba believed she really, simply couldn't take another second, when the pleasure was so intense it nearly became pain—and at that moment he put his lips around her bud and sucked.

Satisfaction tore through her in waves, ebbing and fading only to return again with new strength, while he teased at her slick flesh and she cried out in sheer relief. She was left boneless, shaking, while Rushmore stretched out alongside her and pulled her into the warmth of his embrace.

Hecuba sighed and snuggled closer. The haze of gratification didn't prevent her from noticing that beneath his trousers he was still prodigiously hard. Idly she wondered if he might ask her to do something about that. It could be interesting...

He brushed something gritty from her shoulder with one hand. "An attic floor," he said. "How terribly romantic of me."

"It was your only option," Hecuba replied, her cheek against the soft old linen of his shirt. She was not quite ready to let him go just yet. It was not entirely a comfortable realization. She shivered a little against the chill.

He brushed more dust from her back—paying particular attention to certain lower parts of her—then, to Hecuba's frustration, he rose to his knees beside her. "I shall arrange something better next time," Rushmore promised.

"So there is to be a next time," Hecuba said. Her discomfort evaporated like dew beneath the sun. She stood and padded behind the screen where her clothes rested.

"We have three more sittings according to the terms of our bargain," he said, following her to the screen and watching while she donned her clothes and restored her hair to decency. He wasn't dodging, surely?

"I wasn't thinking of the sitting but about what happened afterward," Hecuba said. "I assume you, as a man, know of certain ways to prevent me from conceiving? And that you would not hesitate to use them?"

He nodded.

"Good," Hecuba said. "That makes things much simpler in the long run."

"I agree," Rushmore said. With a single guttering candle, he guided her back down the stairs and to a convenient side door, providing her with a key to the lock, which was a thoughtful touch. Before Hecuba turned the corner, she allowed herself one glance back at the window where Rushmore stood sentry. The lone candle glinted like a lighthouse on some faraway shore.

Hecuba shook off the fancy and vanished into the darkness.

CHAPTER 5

*F*or the next two days and nights, John lived in a waking dream.

Memories flashed continually before him: Hecuba's skin in candlelight, Hecuba swathed in green, her warrior's poise, her menacing figure as Circe, the sound of her fluent cursing and the taste of her pleasure on his tongue. With these images came other visions, daydreams and allegories, all making his hands itch to be working as he went dazedly through his normal social rounds. He had been inspired after that first kiss—or had it been the second? —but that had been but a pale shadow of the urges that drove him now.

When on the second evening he found himself seated three rows behind Hecuba at a musicale, he found it difficult to convince himself she was really, physically present and not simply a figment of his overzealous imagination. He spent the whole time staring at the line of her neck and the arrangement of her hair, some complicated whirl of red strands, curled and pinned. Her gown was a delicate ivory and seemed likely to have been originally made for her rosy, dark-haired cousin, as the color made Hecuba herself look wan and ghostly. She disappeared with her aunt and uncle shortly after the performance ended, which only added to John's impression of otherworldliness. He'd gone home and immediately filled several sheets with images of her turning her head, craning her neck or leaning forward to better hear the music.

And tonight she was due to return.

He knew better than to imagine, as some men did, that he could simply slake his desires with one riotous fuck and move on. It would be like a man dying of thirst thinking he could save himself by plunging off a cliff and into the sea—merely a different danger. Nor did he imagine that fucking Hecuba would be anything less than life-changing. She'd nearly sent him up in flames the other night and remembering it only made him burn more. Physical pleasure had not been unknown in his life, but it had never taken him with such force before. He'd poured this longing into his art, and the results had been immeasurably gratifying.

Of course that begged the question: if he spent all that energy in bed with his muse, would there be any left for his painting?

It was that fear that had compelled him to remain clothed the other night, even as he had indulged his need to enjoy her, just a little. John knew that he would not be able to resist temptation a second time—especially since the lady herself seemed quite determined to be debauched.

It was inevitable, John decided at last. He exerted himself to finish as many sketches and studies as he could before the well went dry and decided to paint something wildly ambitious before he let himself burn on the sacrificial pyre.

So when Hecuba Jones arrived in the north attic on that fateful night, she walked into a room transformed.

Circe was leaning against one wall, set aside until it had dried enough for John to add finer details and highlights in a richer layer of paint. A stack of prepared canvases lay beside it. Most of the other sketches and papers had been tidied away, so previously mysterious hulks were revealed to be an old desk, an armchair and a divan with fraying upholstery. The green wool blanket from the earl's study had been spread in the center of the floor and spectacularly lit by the combination of an enormous candelabra and a strategically tilted mirror. A broad basin of water lay at the base of the mirror so that the rippling of the water was reflected back over the wool in waves of eddying light. John was working at his easel, filling in the background—a shadowed forest in green and gray, crowded with mournful willows and ethereal birches. A deep pond lurked ominously on the left-hand side, ringed by a sheltering stand of trees.

The thief walked over and considered the scene with a wrinkle of her nose. "Tell me you're not going to turn me into Ophelia."

John shook his head. "You don't strike me as the type to go mad because some waffling prince throws you over."

"I'm not," she replied, her satisfaction evident.

"You strike me as the type to take what you want, when you want it badly enough," John continued equably.

She looked at him with narrowed eyes. John entertained a fleeting notion to paint her as some imperial assassin, sly and strong and bristling with filigreed blades. "That does not sound like a compliment, Rushmore."

"But is it inaccurate, Jones?" His name on her lips without the formal prefix caused an alarming surge in his blood—he wanted to confirm the growing intimacy between them, but her Christian name once spoken aloud would ensnare him, he was certain. The more so since her Christian name was so very pagan. He wondered if she had been wild and witchlike from birth or if she had merely felt compelled to live up to the ancient name her parents had given her.

Hecuba's mouth turned up at the corners. "Jones," she repeated. "I quite like that." Her smile warmed further as she continued to look up at him in the candlelight.

John's mouth went dry and he was suddenly intensely conscious of how thin a barrier a mere shirt was against a woman like Hecuba Jones. And this was a virginal Hecuba. What would she be like once she knew precisely what pleasures a man's body could bring her? John was petrified by the idea, in more than one sense.

He took a steadying breath and shook off his reverie. He would deal with that complication later. For this last brief window of time, he must think more about art than about her. "I'm going to make you a naiad," he said.

She raised a skeptical eyebrow. "A water nymph?"

"Yes—specifically, the nymph who seduces young Hylas and drowns him while trying to love him." He pointed toward a mossy bank on the right side of the painting, where a nearly nude youth reclined on one elbow. A leopard skin thrown over his hips was his only concession to decency. His hunter's spear was tumbling from his hand as he stared in astonished surprise at absolutely nothing on the pond's edge.

Hecuba leaned closer to the canvas. "Rushmore," she said, looking at the painted man's face, "is that *you*?"

John felt a dull flush clamber up the back of his neck at the amusement in her tone. "I hadn't the time to secure the services of a male model, and I have always been more comfortable painting from life." He gestured at the figure of Hylas, as if he could wave her knowing glance aside as easily. "I tried to make his features more youthful and perfect than my own, but I'm not quite sure if I succeeded. He needs to be someone worth taking advantage of— someone so helpless and beautiful that abducting him is plausible."

Hecuba's gaze flickered over John from neck to knees. She might as well have run her hand over the length of him, the way his body responded to that look. She turned back to the painting with an air of speculation, as though comparing the nudity there with what John's current clothing offered. "He doesn't look helpless: he looks ready," she said. "Look at the tension in his thighs, the way he's half-rising from the ground—he isn't running away, he's running *toward*." She smiled. "Poor boy."

The fond tone and the latent heat in her expression galvanized John. It was just the expression he needed for the painting.

It also made him want to throw her to the floor and fuck her until she screamed his name.

But he couldn't do both—he had to choose one. "I've taken the liberty of selecting a costume."

She followed him behind the screen, where he'd unearthed a bundle from some long-forgotten theatrical something or other. The gown was a froth of ivory fabric covered with layers of sequins and netting and tulle in shades of teal and turquoise. The whole mess fluttered like a trapped butterfly between his outstretched hands. "It's a little more complicated than the last one," he said in apology.

Hecuba stared at it for a long moment as though he'd offered her a rotten apple from the ground beneath the tree. "No," she said at last.

Disappointment pricked at him like a thorn in the side. "Because it makes you look too exposed?" he guessed.

She rejected that with a most unladylike noise. "Because it's too ballerina-pretty," she replied. Her expression was frank. "Do you want me to be a monster or don't you?"

John found himself speechless. Hecuba took the glittering thing from his slackened grip and began turning it this way and that, sifting through the diaphanous layers. "Naiads are supposed to be pretty," he stammered.

She made that sound again, an earthy grunt of rejection that against all expectation sent the blood rushing to his cock. "This one is also supposed to be fatal. She pursues her own pleasure to the point where it destroys an innocent young man." She knelt and spread the costume out on the attic floor then glanced up at him. "May I make some slight alterations?"

John swallowed half a dozen perilous suggestions for other things she might do from that position. "Please," he said simply.

Hecuba gripped one shimmering turquoise panel of tulle and pulled.

With a shearing sound, the small panel tore away from the rest of the costume. She found more pieces in the same shade, ripped them out and lay them to one side. When she'd found all that she could in the mass of fabric, she put the despoiled garment back behind the screen and took her plundered scraps to the basin beside the mirror.

With a casual, matter-of-fact gesture, Hecuba pulled her black shirt over her head.

John stood rooted to the spot.

She loosened her hair from its chignon, tucking pins into her trouser pocket, until soft waves fell around her shoulders, the ends curling flame-bright against the pale linen of her chemise.

Breathing became a Herculean labor and John clenched his fists hard enough to drive his own nails into his palms. Only that spike of pain kept him from reaching out for her.

Hecuba dipped her hands in the basin and ran wet fingers through her hair until the locks were dripping and twisted around one another. Reflected ripples danced over her kneeling form as she picked up the tulle scraps, soaked them and draped them over her upper body—bare shoulders, arms and the long line of her collarbone.

She turned suddenly to face him, palms flat on the planked wooden floor, elbows bent, head low and menacing. Droplets of water streamed through the hair at her temples while the colored netting made her skin shimmer, wraithlike and weird in the undulating radiance from the mirror. The tulle's sequins became scales, winking treacherously in the watery light.

A jolt shook him. Had her eyes always been green or was it simply a trick of the light?

John was suddenly stretched taut as though he were tearing free of an old skin long outworn. "*Don't move,*" he commanded and leapt back to his easel and the paints he'd spent so long preparing.

She disobeyed, turning slightly as he changed positions so that when he reached the easel she was still facing him. John was too enraptured to thank her and all but threw himself at the canvas.

He began with the pale colors—shoulders and arms in

gleaming ivory with hints of eerie green overtones. He gave in to temptation and allowed his brush to trace the curves of her breast and even point out one delicate, dark nipple, knowing he could paint her into modesty later if she asked him to. The scale-sequins glittered, sleek and pointed, alluring to the eye but knife-edged for the unwary.

John picked up a fresh brush and loaded it with both chrome orange and Indian yellow—not so they mixed, but so they unrolled in tandem as the paint flowed onto the canvas—and traced the sinuous curls of wet hair on her brow and down the back of her neck. They hugged her arms like snakes, making her as much Medusa as nymph. He would add other layers later, glazing to make some areas darker and scumbling others lighter for highlights and contrast.

When he finally stopped for breath, a reasonable facsimile of Hecuba Jones was just emerging from the painted pond, water lapping at her waist, an alluring smile on her face and a determined light in her eyes. But the appearance of the nymph meant Hylas' face had to change as well—James took his finest brush and made a few careful alterations. The youth was now more spellbound than shocked, wondering rather than terrified.

John glanced back at the real Hecuba just in time to see her shiver. If he hadn't been observing her so closely for such a length of time, he'd never have caught it.

He put his brush down at once, appalled by his lack of thought. "Your patience verges on saintly, Jones," he said, walking over to kneel beside her. "Please know that you can ask for a respite at any time." With careful hands he removed the chilled, damp tulle from her shoulders. Her skin was cool beneath his hands and her chemise had gone nearly transparent with water from her hair. John ignored this temptation, shook the dust from the blanket on the ground and bundled her in green wool—not without a nostalgic pang. He was never going to be able to look at this blanket the same way again.

"Thank you," said Hecuba then shivered again.

Mildly alarmed, John pulled her into his lap.

She wriggled closer and made a sound—such a sound!—in the back of her throat. It was just the sort of pleased, pleasured groan a water-veined nymph might have made when clasped by the warm-blooded arms of a living mortal man. The sound threw caution and art right out of John's head and replaced them with memories of sweet-scented flesh and tangled limbs.

"There's a fire downstairs," he blurted. Hecuba's eyes widened. "In my bedroom," John clarified. "For you."

Hecuba blinked—and just as John realized how gauche he'd sounded, she started to shake with helpless, wrenching laughter. "It's a boon for humanity that you are a painter and not a poet," she chortled.

The trembling motion of her body while she laughed proved to be the final straw for John's perishing self-control. He plunged one hand into her still-damp hair and brushed his mouth against her cheek.

Hecuba went still. John teased his way to the hollow below her ear, flicking his tongue out occasionally to catch droplets as they passed across her skin. "It's always water with you," he said. "First the rain and now this." She hummed and tilted her head to the side, offering him more. He kissed along the line of her neck and startled a gasp from her with a gentle scrape of his teeth. Meanwhile his hands spread across the width of her back, slipping beneath the blanket to rest against the steel in her spine.

"Tell me, Jones," he murmured, "do you still mean to have me?"

"Yes," she said.

He smiled and pulled her up. "Let me show you the way."

CHAPTER 6

*S*he retrieved her lost shirt while he extinguished all but one of the candles. It was a meager light but it guided them well enough down the main stairs. They moved softly to make certain none of the household were stirring. Her hand in his had warmed now, a bold and possessive pressure as he led her along a carpeted hallway and opened the door of his bedchamber.

He pulled the door shut with a click, extinguished the candle, walked to the hearth and stirred the waiting flames into a blaze. When he finally turned around, Hecuba was bending close to the wall to examine part of the pattern of the wallpaper, an expression of wonder on her face. The draping blanket and her leaning posture made her look like a mysterious old woman from a fairy tale, the kind who helps the virtuous and curses the cruel.

"How old were you when you did this?" she whispered.

John smiled as she scrutinized the outline of a knight-errant mounted on a white horse that his younger self had repainted with zebra stripes. "I was just turned twelve," he said, "and I stole my sister's paints to do it. My mother was livid but my father merely laughed and said he would find someone to give me lessons. 'If you're going to do the thing, you may as well do it properly,' he said."

Hecuba smiled at a housecat he'd turned into a tiger; the beast prowled beside a tulip that had sprouted two pink ankles to become the tumultuous upflung skirts of a tumbling lady. Her eyes briefly met John's, warm and conspiratorial. "You do the thing very properly indeed," she said.

She was the daughter of a painter—a genius—and with a nasty jolt John realized that he didn't know whether she was attracted to him more for his work or for himself. He'd put so much of himself into his art that he had never really thought to make the distinction before. Not until Hecuba Jones had come along and split him in two. Now the gentle movement of her fingers over that tin-plate hero made jealousy bubble up within his heart, a slimy, tentacled monster in the deep.

But judging by how she'd stared at Hylas, he had certain aesthetic advantages, if he were brave enough to employ them.

With deliberate, unhurried hands, John unbuttoned his cuffs and pulled the charcoal- and paint-stained shirt over his head.

As he cast the garment to the floor, he noticed that he'd succeeded in diverting her from the wallpaper. Hecuba Jones had straightened to her full height again and was watching him with an avid gleam in her eyes.

John held out one hand.

"Oh no," said Hecuba with a shake of her head. "You've already seen me naked. I'm going to insist that you finish disrobing before I get any nearer."

It only took a single step for John to reach her. "Indeed?" he said, grasping the edge of the blanket and pulling her closer.

She stopped him with a hand on his chest. He savored the feel of her fingers spread out against him. "Indeed," she said. Her voice softened. "I want to look at you. All of you."

John took a deep breath and stepped back, but kept his hold on the blanket. Hecuba was compelled to follow him.

One more step back and John was able to sit down on the bed. Hecuba stood before him, candlelight dancing in her eyes, half-dry hair tumbling around her shoulders. He let go of the blanket and lifted one foot onto the bed, sliding the white sock down from beneath his trouser hem.

Hecuba licked her lips and John had to catch his breath. From just removing a shirt and a sock! What would happen once every scrap of cloth was gone between them?

John removed the other sock and put his feet back on the floor. The carpet felt impossibly soft against his bare soles.

He'd had women tease him this way before but he'd never taken such time with the removal of his own garb. He was far more comfortable observing than being observed—but somehow the strangeness now was exhilarating. Beneath her gaze, the hair on his naked skin prickled with awareness. He watched her watching him and desire curled low and hot in his belly.

John put his hands to the fall of his trousers, undoing them in as leisurely a manner as he could stand. He rose as he pushed them down his hips. They rustled and fell to the floor along with his smallclothes, and finally he stood in all his glory before the scrutiny of Hecuba Jones. The crackle of the fire in the grate made a mockery of how cool the air felt, an invisible caress on his overheated skin and jutting cock.

She took her time looking him up and down before raising her eyes to meet his again. "That was a very accurate self-portrait upstairs," Hecuba murmured.

John bowed his head at the double compliment, more embarrassed to be blushing than to be naked.

Hecuba slipped the blanket from her shoulders and it fell to the floor. She removed nothing else, merely stepped closer and—finally—began to touch him.

It was everything he'd wanted and more, her fingers like tongues of flame against his flesh. She smoothed her palms along lines of muscle and dragged her fingertips over his nipples, which hardened at once for her. It required every ounce of John's restraint to keep still and not reach out to touch her in return, but he bit his tongue and reminded himself that she was untried and it was best to let her take things at whatever speed she willed.

Later, he hoped, there would be nights when she would allow him to do the same. Tonight he was entirely hers.

She leaned forward and pressed her mouth to the base of his neck.

It was precisely the same kiss that had once made him beg her to wait. It had the opposite effect now. John felt as though every vein in his body lit up, drawing heat from her mouth like signal fires along a series of mountain peaks. His cock, already hard, stiffened nearly to the point of pain—and still his hands remained at his sides, though now they shook with the effort of holding back.

One of Hecuba's hands trailed down his hip, over bone and tendon, to the sensitive skin of his thigh. She lingered there, either teasing or timid—John didn't much care which—until a definitive motion brought her hand into contact with his shaft.

John's eyes twisted shut and he shivered.

At first she merely caressed him with the same slow tempo she'd used on every other part of him. But then her hand closed tight and hot around him, and a single bold stroke tore a groan from his throat.

"You're far more patient than I had anticipated," said Hecuba.

John opened his eyes to the mind-melting sight of Hecuba Jones with his cock in her hand and an impudent grin on her face.

He let out such a filthy curse that even Hecuba gasped, a shocked rush of air that curled over his lips as he claimed her mouth. She slid her tongue against his as he pulled her tight against him, the cloth of her trousers a delicious friction against his aching cock. She twined her arms around his waist and he fisted his hands in her hair as the kiss turned dark, almost feral—the wet curl of tongues, the velvet yield of lips, the bright, sharp notes of teeth.

Then Hecuba Jones took his lower lip between her teeth and bit down—not hard, but not gently either.

One moment they were standing, straining together. The next they were tangled in the bedclothes, sprawled at an angle across the expanse of the bed, still entwined, still kissing. John had no idea how they'd gotten there. He had a vague memory that he had thrown her down and himself along with her. There was no time now to sort out what had happened, because his fingers were already slipping beneath the hem of that provocative chemise and pulling it up to bare her breasts. He left the linen gathered around her shoulders, bent his head and sucked one sweet nipple into his mouth.

Hecuba moaned and closed her eyes even as her hands went to work on the buttons of her trousers. John moved to her other nipple, cupping her breast in the heat of his palm and blowing gently across the wetness left by his mouth.

Hecuba opened her eyes when she failed to open her trousers quickly enough. "Damn buttons," she muttered, still working to undo them. John laughed and put his hands down to help. Together, gracelessly, they wrestled the bulky garment down to her ankles and away. Her pantalets, however, were still tied around her waist.

Hecuba was left in nothing but white linen and black stockings.

John froze at this vision. Not of innocence—her red hair was too wild, her breasts still naked, her stockings black as night. But there was some quality in her that insisted on shining through and amplifying the effect of whatever she happened to be wearing. Or not wearing. It was that same quality that drew him to try to replicate her likeness on the page over and over again, the same thing that he sensed would constantly bewitch him, whether five or fifty or a hundred years went by.

In his bed, she lounged on her elbows like a goddess of classical antiquity, a creature of light and flame and shadow all at once. Purely and completely herself.

When he was still wordless and wondering, she put a hand to his cheek. "Second thoughts?" she asked, not quite hiding her anxiety.

It was a fair question and one he'd answered differently two nights earlier. Everything had changed since then. He turned and pressed a kiss to her palm, reveling in the gentle pressure of her hand.

Hecuba smiled, relaxed and stroked her thumb against his lips. He tilted his head and bit the end of her thumb. She sucked in a harsh breath and her eyes went dark.

John leaned down to kiss her again, his body bearing hers down into the mattress. White linen shifted against his burning skin like gossamer, an incitement to lust rather than a barrier. Hecuba lifted one leg and wrapped it around his hip. John took advantage of the motion and settled the shaft of his cock against her cleft, blazingly aware of her heat even through the linen. He rocked himself against her, first slowly and then with more force as she writhed and arched beneath him.

Finally it was too much for him. He raised himself away from her, though his senses screamed at the loss, then tugged at the ties to her pantalets.

She took his meaning at once and pulled the rumpled chemise off over her head while he untied the strings and slid the pantalets down from her hips. Hecuba was left wearing nothing but a pair of knee-high black stockings—with matching garters—that only made the rest of her look more profoundly naked by comparison.

John leaned on one elbow looking down at her, torn between the need to take her and the urge to stare. Though he'd had other lovers before—some of them in this very bed—John knew that there was something about this night that was going to mark him even as it marked her. It wasn't simply her first time—it was *their* first time.

She quirked an eyebrow at him and bent one knee. John's mouth went dry. "Does it always take so long to get oneself deflowered?" she asked pointedly.

John laughed. "If you're lucky," he replied, but his smile faded into something more tender. He traced a hand down her side, relishing the curve of her waist, the softness of her. "It's not a thing that happens every day, Jones."

"I'm still wearing my stockings." She reached out.

He stopped her with a hand on her wrist. "Leave them," he said. She looked at him, flushing, while he savored the perfect curves of her silk-clad calves.

He could have stayed that way forever, just looking, but Hecuba had other plans. She framed his face with her hands and kissed him—a sweet, soft kiss that shook him down to his bones.

He stole one hand between her legs and into the springy red curls there. She was already wet—oh God, his cock throbbed at that—but he wanted her more than ready, so he began sliding one thick finger along the cleft of her lower lips, a light rasping friction along her clitoris.

Hecuba spread her legs a little wider and hummed low in her throat, her eyes heavy lidded and glittering in the firelight. John skimmed his lips over her shoulder as he played with her, attuned to even the tiniest intake of her breath. After a little while he leaned over and whispered, "I'm going to use one finger to start."

Eyes closed, Hecuba nodded.

John turned his hand and slowly slid his middle finger into the eager heat of her. Hecuba let out a breathy cry that made him shake, but he pushed his own arousal aside and kept his focus on her.

He began to thrust.

"Oh God." Hecuba groaned. By the third stroke she was already arching her hips up from the bed so John took the hint and increased his pace. She welcomed this, inner walls clasping around him, a flush spreading over her skin. Her breath came faster and faster and she began to tremble. John reached up with his thumb and began stroking her clitoris in time with the movements of his finger.

Hecuba came, one hand fisted in the bedclothes, the other clasped tight against her mouth to muffle her cries. John nearly spent himself at the sight.

And then...a tear slipped down her cheek.

John went dizzy with shock. He forgot his pleasure in her

pleasure and his own still-unsatisfied desire. His finger slipped free of her body and he pulled her into his arms. "What's wrong?" he whispered as she wrapped her arms around him and held tight.

"I couldn't hold back," she said, the dark weight of regret in her voice.

John rubbed soothing circles between her shoulder blades. "Oh, Jones," he sighed, relief and realization mingled. "You don't have to hold back."

"I didn't want it to be over," she continued, her voice muffled against his chest.

"It isn't over," John said. "Far from it." She pulled her head away to stare up at him and he couldn't help the knowing smile that lifted his lips. "Jones," he said, "don't you know you can do it again?"

She looked startled—then intrigued. "Prove it," she demanded.

It occurred to John, as his cock sprang immediately back to attention, that he had waited far too long to take Hecuba Jones to his bed.

How many times did a woman have to ask him to fuck her?

She hadn't used that precise word, of course—though he had a marked suspicion she could have—but she'd made her desires plain enough. And he'd been holding back, lurching forward, then pulling back again, like an untrained horse in harness.

Well, no longer.

So he rose from the bed, found one of the sheaths he'd procured and slipped it over his cock, tying the ribbon tight at the base. Hecuba's eyes were on him the whole time, which added an exhibitionist charge to the process. He felt like a courtesan posing for her protector.

It was unsettling to realize that he liked the feeling.

He was beginning to think he would like anything as long as it involved Hecuba Jones and a bed. And the bed was probably optional.

She opened her arms to him as he returned to her warmth. The touch of her skin set him alight again—he needed to be inside her more than he needed his next breath. He pushed his hips between her thighs, rough, at the limits of his patience, but she merely spread her legs wide to accommodate him. He set the head of his cock at her entrance and scraped up enough self-control to meet her gaze before he went any further.

She laughed and tugged at his shoulders. Had any woman ever been so amused by her own seduction? "Now," she insisted.

John obligingly began to push forward.

The briefest of resistances and he was past her maidenhead. Hot and tight and oh so slick—her gasp and his groan came simultaneously. She stretched around him and he clenched his hands in the sheets to keep from pounding mindlessly into her. *That can come later*, whispered a treacherous voice in his head. It sent a frisson of pure need spiraling down to the base of his spine and he pushed in another inch.

Hecuba raised her thighs higher and wrapped her legs around his waist.

John lost control of himself and plunged in to the hilt.

"Hell!" Hecuba swore.

John shuddered and felt his cock throb inside her. He didn't know how long he could keep himself from moving. "Sorry," he ground out. "Too rough."

"No," she corrected him on a moan, "I like it."

Those three small words were all it took to break him. John's mouth came down harshly on hers as he began to move. Her stocking feet rasped lightly against the skin of his hips while he drove his cock home with long, powerful strokes—a driving rhythm some reasonable part of him worried was too much for a recent virgin. But that same recent virgin just slid her hands up to the back of his neck for leverage and met him stroke for stroke, breasts shaking with every desperate thrust.

The reasonable part of him vanished.

He tore his mouth from hers and buried his face in her neck, the better to fuck her as hard as he needed to. She bit down on his shoulder as he pistoned into her, her inner muscles working him and her hands pulling his hair just hard enough for the feeling to stand out in the sea of pleasure. Sweat gathered in the hollow above his buttocks as he strove for his long-denied climax.

Hecuba released his shoulder and panted against his ear. "I'm close," she said. "So close. But I don't... I can't..." A wordless cry of frustration shook her beneath him.

Through his haze, John realized what she needed. He was too far gone himself for dexterity—but he could use her boldness to both their advantage.

With an effort, he pushed his arms straight to either side, palms flat on the bed, making a space between their torsos even as he continued to thrust inside her. "Go on," he rumbled, his jaw clenched tight against the urge to come at the sight of her flesh, pink and stretched around him. "Take what you need."

With only the briefest hesitation, she slid one hand down to where they were joined. It took her a moment, but he knew she'd found the right spot when she gasped and her hand began to move in time with his needy cock.

The sight of her stroking herself while he fucked her seared into him like a brand. He sped up, so close to the edge he could almost taste it, then gave one particularly rough thrust that drove him impossibly deep within the throbbing, slippery warmth of her cunt.

Hecuba came so hard she curled up around him, clutching at his shoulders with her free hand and panting desperately against the crook of his neck. It was too much—he'd been holding back too long. With a hoarse cry, John followed her up and over the edge, into flight, pulsing and shaking as he poured himself into her quivering body and sparks burst in the darkness behind his eyes.

Slowly the aftershocks died away and their bodies regained their accustomed weight. John ran wondering hands down the curves of her hips and along the stockings she still wore, the black silk impossibly dark against the sheets. There were holes in them, he noticed now—spots where her skin showed through in delightfully lurid circles. He wanted to slip those stockings down over her calves, her ankles—remove them entirely and use them tie her down beneath him in the bed. Or else let her tie *him* up…Yes, he rather thought she would enjoy that.

Hecuba sat up with a sigh and reached for her pantalets. "I must be going."

There was regret in her voice but not enough of it to soothe the sting. "When will you come back?" he asked, striving to keep his voice level and calm. Damn it all, she'd been the virgin, so why did he feel as though he'd lost something tonight?

She pulled on her white chemise and smiled mischievously at him over her shoulder. Her lips were pink, her cheeks still flushed from climax, her hair tumbled and wilder than ever. *Circe again*, he thought, *rising from the bed of Odysseus*. His hands shook with the need to reach for a pencil and sheet of paper even as his body hummed with exhaustion. Apparently fucking Hecuba Jones as hard as he could had done nothing to curb his impulse to capture her image. He couldn't wait to paint her again. And to fuck her again.

He lay dazed by these twin revelations while Hecuba once again put on her black thief's garb. It was only as she pinned up her hair that he recalled his promise to her. "Wait," he said. He threw on a dressing gown, retrieved *Hecuba as Henry VIII* from his wardrobe—still in its protective roll, still bound by his cravat—and held it out to her. "We'll be even after this," he said.

Hecuba took her mother's painting but her eyes flashed up at him. "There are still two more paintings you have that I want," she reminded him.

John braced himself against the tide of relief. "Two more nights?" he said.

"Two more nights," Hecuba agreed.

CHAPTER 7

*H*ecuba had never known two days could take so long to pass.

It didn't help that recent activities had left her sore in some unwonted places. Every time she took a step or sat down, the quiet ache between her legs brought visions of Rushmore's hands and mouth and hips, the feeling of his muscular body moving against hers, the pleasures that could be gleaned from a sensitive man with a ready cock. She knew better than to reveal these secrets to her family, particularly her innocent cousins—though there was a speculative gleam in Anne's eyes every now and again when she looked at a gentleman, which made Hecuba suspect her cousin would not be as shocked as a maiden ought to be.

So she held her tongue through all the visits for tea, shopping expeditions, a walk along the Serpentine, dinner *en famille* and luncheon with Aunt Eleanor's circle of invariably hen-like acquaintances. It was downright disheartening to find that her continuous, deliberate silence went unremarked by everyone.

Well, nearly everyone.

At home on the afternoon of the second day, Anne poured tea then took a seat beside Hecuba. On the other side of the room

Aunt Eleanor and Mrs. Gunn leaned close in a confederacy of gossip. Evangeline was sitting beside them, blushing and smiling and nervous.

Anne, however, was perfectly confident when she asked her cousin, "Are you going to tell me what the matter is?"

Hecuba blinked in surprise. "What?" she asked, genuinely confounded.

Anne snorted. "You've not said a word in two days. Mother has noticed and is somewhat relieved—she thinks you've finally learned proper feminine docility—but you haven't said anything to me or to Evangeline either, and that isn't like you. Also, Dorothy told me that some nights it looks as though your bed hasn't been slept in."

Hecuba froze with the teacup halfway to her mouth.

Anne peered at her with narrowed eyes. "Dorothy's right—you haven't been sleeping well, have you? You have such dark circles beneath your eyes."

Hecuba silently cursed herself for a fool. She ought to have thought to muss the bedclothes a little upon returning to her aunt and uncle's house. Damn Rushmore and his distractions. But Anne had that set to her mouth that told Hecuba she wouldn't be put off without answers. "You're right," she said, thinking quickly. "I haven't slept well at all this week." It had the benefit of being true—but Anne, though she nodded sympathetically, would need more than that to be satisfied. "Do you remember those four paintings that used to hang in the parlor at the cottage, before my parents died?"

"The portraits?" Anne asked. Hecuba nodded. "I always liked those, especially the one of your mother. Whatever happened to them?"

"Your father sold them," Hecuba said bluntly.

Anne had the grace to look shocked. "But...the will said those were to stay in the family. I mean—that is—they were family portraits!"

"And now they belong to the Earl of Underwood's younger brother."

"Good God." Anne fell backward against the over-upholstered back of the chair. "No wonder you were so snappish when we introduced you." She glanced at Evangeline, who was straining to hear her sister and cousin's conversation, and lowered her voice. "However did you find out?"

Hecuba spoke as low as she could while Anne took a leisurely sip of tea to mask her avid interest from Evangeline and Aunt Eleanor. "Your father kept putting me off when I asked about the paintings, so I picked the lock on his desk and found a bill of sale dated last spring."

Anne choked on her tea. She set the cup aside and coughed a little into her hand. When she could speak again, her voice was rough. "He used the money to pay for our Season." It was not a question.

Hecuba inclined her head. She'd come to the same conclusion.

Anne's mouth tightened into a grim line. "And now you're wearing my castoffs while Evangeline and I have new wardrobes bought with funds that by rights belong to you." The wave of her hand took in both her own pale-pink gown, expertly ruffled, and Hecuba's ivory muslin, the pale hue of which made her look as though she were the victim of an intestinal complaint.

"You didn't seem to mind before," Hecuba couldn't help pointing out.

Anne turned her teacup around and around on its saucer. "You made it plain you thought the whole thing was a waste of time and effort, that you had no desire to—how did you put it?—to be dragged to the altar like a sacrificial lamb." She put aside the teacup and met her cousin's gaze frankly. "I do want to be married, you see. I want children and a home of my own. A London Season is the best chance I have of getting that."

"I know," Hecuba said. On impulse she reached out and took Anne by the hand. "And I don't resent you for wanting something different for your life. I just wish..."

"I do too," Anne replied when Hecuba trailed off. She squeezed her cousin's hand and the light of trouble kindled in her eyes. "Do you think you might teach me how to pick locks?" she asked.

Hecuba agreed with a grin, thrilled both to have made an ally and because she had succeeded in distracting Anne from her original line of inquiry.

She took pains to disarrange the bedclothes thoroughly that night before slipping out on her way to the Earl of Underwood's townhouse.

Rushmore wasn't waiting downstairs for her, but that was hardly an obstacle. She found the subtle door and the servant's stair that led to the north attic. He wasn't there either—but he'd left a candle burning, and beside it a note with her name in a script too rushed for elegance.

She picked up the letter.

Jones,

If you're reading this, some tedious evening affair has gone on far longer than necessary. I will be with you as soon as I possibly can.

Yours, Rushmore

Hecuba looked for a long time at that single word. *Yours.* She wasn't quite certain what to do with it. Was he hers, really? After so short an acquaintance, however intense? Did it mean that he considered her *his* in some similar way? She didn't feel as though she belonged to anyone other than herself. And what was she? A fortuneless miss of questionable birth, plainspoken and suspicious and only half-civilized. Whereas John Rushmore had a magnetism about him that could increasingly pull her off course, or cause her natural hue to fade like bright pigments left out in too-strong sun.

No. They had made a bargain and that would be that: four sittings, four paintings, with four passionate nights to follow. Then she would have her mother's paintings...and with them, the key. Then Hecuba could build her own life, independent of her aunt and uncle and the ever more oppressive strictures of polite society.

Yours.

Did Rushmore really believe there could be something long-lasting between them? She would miss him, certainly, when she left—she would even cry, no doubt—but their futures led down very different paths. Hers would take her to a life no gentleman would countenance, especially not one who was next in line for an earldom, with all the responsibilities and privileges that entailed.

There was no use hoping for anything more than what they had. The sharp dismay that had begun to strike whenever she thought of their parting was a symptom of sentiment, not a guide for future action.

Perhaps Rushmore's artistic tendencies were running away with his better sense. Perhaps she was overthinking this.

She folded the note and set it aside.

She would give him half an hour, no more.

Hecuba took the candle over to where the two previous paintings leaned, facing the attic wall to shield the paint from the sun while they dried. *Circe* was even more mesmerizing now than it had been at first: Rushmore had used his most delicate brush to add detail to the original scene, honing the expression on her face and bringing the cup in her hand to vivid life. She put it carefully back and turned to examine the second painting, which she had not actually seen at their previous meeting.

She gasped and nearly dropped the candle.

On canvas her body shimmered with scales in some places and gleamed like pearl in others, particularly the naked breasts so obviously painted by a lover's hand. He'd made her hair a shade darker—or perhaps that had been the water—and against the green of the background it burned like a flame. Her expression was patently hungry, bright of eye and red of lip, and with a jolt Hecuba saw that her presence in the painting had transformed Hylas. That young, doomed man was now all eagerness, trembling and ready to throw himself into the depths for one touch of that water creature's hand.

A footstep on the stair alerted her to Rushmore's approach. He was resplendent in black formal dress, the snowy front of his cravat shining like a star in the dim light. "My apologies, Jones," he said then his brow furrowed and he came closer. "I hope you haven't been waiting too long?"

Hecuba's throat was too full to speak at first so she merely gestured at the naiad in the painting.

"Ah." Rushmore traced one hand along the edge of the canvas. "I did some more work on that one this afternoon. What do you think?"

It felt as though the words were torn from somewhere deep within her. "You made me beautiful," she said.

John was silent for so long that eventually she had to look up at him. He was staring at her as if she were daft. "I paint what I see."

Hecuba held the candle up to better see his face. His expression was solemn, if a bit puzzled, and his eyes were clear and earnest.

The realization that he was serious about her beauty staggered her.

Seeking the comforting mask of darkness, Hecuba turned her head and extinguished the light with a breath, then set the candle aside. Her fingers first found Rushmore's cravat, a ghostly white in the dimness, then traced the steely line of his jaw and the softer skin of his cheeks. She rose on tiptoe to feather her lips along his, keeping her motions light and delicate. Slowly she began to deepen the kiss, but still it was a fragile thing, born of gratitude and wonder.

Rushmore sighed into her mouth but his hands stayed at his sides. There was sherry on his breath and the smallest hint of a cheroot, bitter and sharp. In the dark it was easy to believe she was as beautiful as he seemed to think, that she had all those powers of attraction she'd never dared to claim for herself. That the sight of her could cause a man to risk his whole future just for the chance to touch her and be touched in return.

"You should take me downstairs," she whispered.

She felt as well as heard him chuckle. "So impatient, Jones?"

She dropped her hands and stepped away, invisible now, the candle still in her pocket. "Or I could leave," she said, the teasing lilt in her voice belying the way her heart was hammering in her breast.

A rush of air and his hands caught her—the sound of her voice had given away her location in the dark. "Never," he said and pulled her up hard against him, his earlier reticence cast aside. One arm banded tight around her waist and the other caught the back of her neck as he slanted his mouth over hers again and again. She kissed him back just as desperately. "You were right," he said, breaking away to take in a lungful of air, "I should take you downstairs."

Hand in hand, they stole like fugitives down to Rushmore's bedroom.

The fire had burned down to embers, the barest pinpricks in the dark room. Hecuba silently shut the door while Rushmore pulled open the curtains, letting the light of the half-moon slip in and dance on every edge in the room: the polished wood of the bedstead, the metal poker by the hearth, the edge of a small shaving mirror on the dresser. Then he was across the room, sliding his hands beneath both her shirt and chemise, feathering her skin with kisses even as he removed the rest of her clothing with practiced efficiency.

He paused when only her black stockings remained then knelt and traced reverent hands up the side of her calf. "God, Jones," he murmured, "do you know how these have tortured me?"

Hecuba squirmed beneath his regard, even in the moon's mild illumination. "They've been darned half a dozen times over, and they've got ladders enough for all of Jacob's angels," she demurred.

Rushmore merely laughed. "Perhaps," he allowed, shaking his head as if this were the most trivial of objections, "but Jones, they're *yours*." His eyes were as bright as the moon when he looked up at her. "Do you think I'd somehow be more overwhelmed if they were brand-new, hand-stitched and straight from Paris?"

Hecuba had no answer for that.

Rushmore leaned over and pressed a kiss to her thigh. His fingers, meanwhile, insinuated themselves beneath the band of her garter. Slowly he slid the old silk down her legs, his dark head bent, his breath warm on her skin. A jolt of power went through Hecuba, a frisson of something potent and energizing.

When she was naked, he looked up at her again with a smile. She reached to pull him up from his knees, but he stopped her, brushing her hands aside.

She could feel that smile still curving his lips when his mouth reached her clitoris. He tongued her delicately, teasingly, his fingertips resting gently on her hips, holding her there as though ensorcelled. Slowly his tongue slipped deeper as he drank from her body, the dark rhythm he set spiraling through her causing her to spread her thighs wider to give him better access. He groaned and pressed closer, the white sliver of his shirt gleaming against the darkness.

Hecuba reveled in every flick of his tongue and movement of his lips, but it soon became clear to her that this steady pace would make climax elusive and unattainable. She tightened her hands on the collar of his dark coat, pulling his head up from between her legs. His amusement was evident in the arch of his eyebrows and the quirk at the corners of his mouth.

That mouth sparked some rebellious flame in her soul, stirred up by unsatisfied arousal and the determination not to let him have it all his own way. She sank down to the floor with him, straddling his trousered hips and thrusting her hands beneath the cloth of his black coat. Her mouth claimed his and kept him occupied while her hands pulled the coat from his shoulders, down his arms to his wrists. She arched her hips in a teasing stroke and felt him gasp into her mouth; at the same time, she twisted the fabric of the coat tightly in one hand, effectively pinioning his arms behind him.

Rushmore realized what had happened and went still—except for his cock, which twitched even beneath the fabric layers that separated them.

Hecuba smiled, though the shadows were deeper down here than they'd been when she was standing. She knew very well Rushmore could break her hold if he truly wanted to, but he didn't. His every muscle was tensed, thighs taut beneath her, his breath a harsh sound against the soft night air. Hecuba's pulse ticked slightly upward. This was new, and very interesting.

She leaned in to brush her lips against Rushmore's ear, while with her free hand she began unraveling the knot at his neck. "That's two of your cravats I have now," she said, pulling the linen free.

"Where is the other?" Rushmore asked.

"In my trouser pocket, wrinkling itself to death," Hecuba said, her hand busy on the fine gold buttons of his waistcoat. She pressed her mouth to the side of his neck and admitted, "I didn't dare to ask the servants to clean and press it." He gave a low moan that turned to a gasp when she scraped him with her teeth. "What on earth would I be doing with a gentleman's cravat?"

"For one thing," Rushmore said, low and intense, "you could tie it around my wrists instead of the coat."

Hecuba looked at his face, shrouded in darkness. "Would that please you?"

"Would it please you to have me at your mercy?" he countered.

Hecuba slid her hand down and squeezed his cock where it tented up from his trousers. Rushmore made a strangled sound as his head fell back.

"Aren't you at my mercy already?" she teased.

In the darkness, with the light behind him, it seemed he moved more swiftly than humanly possible. In one breath he pulled his hands free of the coat and her grip, heaved her up from the floor and tumbled her onto the bed. Hecuba barely had time to gasp in surprise before she was pinned facedown beneath him.

Another moment after that, he'd pulled the cravat from her clutching fingers and knotted it firmly around both the bedpost and her right wrist.

A roaring filled her ears and the blood surged in her veins. *Danger*, she sang to herself and was surprised to feel an echo of that word throb between her legs. She could feel that greedy part of herself growing even wetter at the tension in her bound arm, the feel of the sheets against her bare breasts and the warmth of his breath on the back of her neck. It made her shiver deliciously.

Experimentally she pushed herself up with her other hand, only to stop when her bare back met his semi-clothed chest. "You missed your chance to be in command," he said, and, dear heavens, when he bit lightly at the back of her neck she felt it in every inch of her body.

"I won't be so lax in future," she breathed. He chuckled briefly in response before a wash of cold air told her he'd moved away. A moment later she felt the second cravat—not around her other wrist, as she'd half expected, but encircling her left ankle. She tugged on her bonds and found that a limited range of motion was possible—if she moved lower on the bed, she could tuck both her knees beneath her, though the position required her to stretch her right arm to its full length.

Fabric sounds caught her attention and Hecuba turned to watch over her shoulder as Rushmore began to shed his clothing. His black trousers fell away like husks from some late-blooming flower, his white shirt and smallclothes luminous in the silver light. Soon those garments too were cast away and he stood in nothing more than his own gleaming skin.

Hecuba realized this was the first time both of them had been completely unclothed. But it was difficult in the low light to fix his image in her mind as intensely as she wanted to. "Could you do me a favor and light a candle, Rushmore?"

"The prisoner should be wary of making requests," he replied in low tones. "Every favor comes at a price." Instead of reaching for the nearby taper, he walked to the fireplace and prodded the sleepy embers into a proper flame, his tall form a shadow against the ruddy light.

Hecuba's mouth went dry. Suddenly she was forcefully conscious of how many muscles it took for her body to pull in a breath. She felt every one of them seize and stiffen at the easy power and dark grace of her lover's silhouette.

With unhurried ease, Rushmore moved away from the hearth, and the shadow became a man once more. Firelight gilded the planes of his chest and the muscles of his flanks as he found a sheath and pulled it onto his cock. Hecuba's fingers twitched with the remembered feel of him, hard and hot against her palm.

Provokingly he stopped by the side of the bed, just out of reach of the hand she'd stretched out to touch him. "Oh no," he teased. "You'll have to be patient, Jones."

Hecuba tamped down a growl of frustration. "You have more than enough patience for both of us," she said. "And you're wasting the hours of the night."

One corner of his mouth lifted at her sharp tone, but he did not laugh. "It does feel like we're perpetually running out of time, doesn't it?" Hecuba steeled herself against the dismay in his voice, which was too near an echo of her own secret fears. He stepped behind her, where he could reach her but she couldn't return the caress. Hecuba opened her mouth to protest again but was soothed when he threaded his fingers into her hair, pulling it free of its confinement and letting it cascade down her shoulders. His mouth followed, tracing a leisurely path on the skin of her back. Hecuba sighed, then groaned when one hand slid around her hips and his fingers found that throbbing, aching place where she needed his touch most desperately.

Rushmore moved behind her on the bed, knees to either side of her hips. His naked chest blanketed her, sending warmth through her every nerve and fiber. His hand never paused in its rhythm. "I could spend hours like this," he murmured as she arched into the stroke of his fingers. "Teasing that lovely cunt of yours, toying with you, seeing just how damn wet and hungry you can be." Hecuba's left hand grasped his knee and held it, firm as an anchor.

She could hear his smile as he continued. "Eventually I'd slide into you, inch by inch, drawing out every tiny mote of pleasure. Seeing how many times I could make you come, losing count and starting over again." He slid one finger into her body and curled it just so. Hecuba gasped and bucked against him. Rushmore made a strangled sound in his throat and nipped at her shoulder then smoothed over the bite with a kiss.

But the mask had slipped. All the teasing speeches in the world couldn't hide the heaving breaths that shook him, or the racing of his pulse where his flesh met hers. Hecuba knew he was as close to the brink as she was. All she had to do was push him just a little.

Without hesitation, Hecuba raked her nails over the skin of his thigh.

Rushmore cursed and lost control.

He slipped his fingers free and drove her forward and down, her bound left leg stretching taut, her right leg splaying wide. His weight kept her pinned, his breath hot on the back of her neck. Hecuba cried out as his cock pushed inside her, sliding along her inner walls, hitting that same spot his finger had found earlier. This—*this*—was what she'd needed. The deep drive forward, the long pull back, the way he sped up when her body clenched down on his shaft.

Hecuba wrapped her bound right hand around the linen and held on tight.

And then Rushmore gave a cry and surged forward, his cock throbbing, his every muscle rigid, choked sounds wrenched from his throat as he came, the warmth of his seed palpable even through the sheath. When he stopped shuddering he slid from her body and untied the cravats. Hecuba, empty and puzzled, turned to watch as he pulled off the soiled sheath. "I'm so sorry, Jones," he said, shaking his head. "You were completely right—I moved too slowly and denied myself for too long."

Every bit of Hecuba's body was still pulsing so she tilted her head at him and asked, "Do we have to be done?"

Rushmore looked up at her, his eyebrows arched in surprise. "I suppose not," he admitted as though the idea were a novelty. Hecuba's legs shifted restlessly and his gaze sharpened. "Not at all, in fact," he said, promise lacing his voice like poison in wine.

And that was how Hecuba Jones found herself flat on her back in the bed, with Rushmore's mouth hot and hungry on her cunt again.

This was not the gentle, semi-worshipful experience from before. There was something fierce and feral about it, a long wild note that found its resonance and echo deep inside Hecuba herself. She arched her hips up hard from the bed and twisted her fingers in his hair, begging shamelessly for more. He responded by plunging two fingers into her channel while his lips closed around her aching clitoris. He held nothing back, and before she knew it her body was clenching and coming in endless, wrenching waves.

Slowly she drifted back into herself, languid and glowing with satisfaction. Rushmore wrapped the blankets around them both and Hecuba curled lazily into the warmth of him. "Stay with me for a while?" he asked.

"Just for a moment," she agreed and closed her eyes against the fading firelight.

CHAPTER 8

*R*osy light, warm skin and hair like fire—John filled his hands and pulled Hecuba smoothly on top of him. She smiled and mumbled something sleepy as she leaned down and kissed him, her fingers sliding down his chest, then lower, her smile as luminous as the morning sunlight...

Morning. Something worrisome ate at the fuzzy edges of his thoughts, undermining his pleasure.

A discreet knock sounded on the door—Vickery, the valet, punctual as ever.

Both people in the bed came shockingly awake. Hecuba dove for her scattered clothing while John lunged for the door just as it began to swing open. He caught the corner and held it firm while the valet blinked owlishly through the six-inch gap.

"Vickery," panted John, "I must insist that you close your eyes."

"Of course, sir," the man murmured and stood calmly with eyes screwed shut while Hecuba yanked on her shirt and trousers.

Thank God his bedroom was only one story higher than the ground. John wrenched the window open and helped to lower Hecuba as far as he could before she leapt lightly to the garden path below. She took the time to flash him one mischievous grin before she vanished around the corner, toward the servants' gate and the alley beyond.

John was left behind like Rapunzel in the tower. He shut the window and, just in case, pulled shut the curtains. "Thank you, Vickery," he said. "You may open your eyes again."

The valet shut the door behind him and began to lay out a set of clothing: buff trousers, red waistcoat and dark brown jacket, John was relieved to see. The valet's former employer, the Marquis of Berthet, had been a confirmed dandy, and every so often John had to reject a color combination as too risky or eye-catching. He preferred to display bright hues in his paintings rather than on his person. "I did not realize that you had taken to hosting visitors so late, sir," said Vickery while John pulled on socks and smallclothes. "Please do not hesitate to ask me if you should need refreshments on such nights. Your guest's identity would of course remain a guarded secret."

John fumbled the shirt he was pulling over his head and had to fight his way through the neck. "Really?" he asked. A suspicion rose within him like smoke. "Was Berthet in the habit of hosting such entertainments?" he asked.

"I couldn't say, sir," Vickery murmured.

"So," said the earl, "who is she?"

John swallowed a mouthful of egg and goggled at his brother, who wore an irksomely knowing grin. "I beg your pardon?"

Simon laughed and slid into the nearest chair at the breakfast table. "The woman who's lately bewitched you of course. Don't pretend there isn't one."

John simply stared, fork tilting down in his slack fingers.

Simon leaned closer to press his point. "One, you've barely ventured out of the house,—not to your club, not to the opera, not even to the homes of your bohemian friends. Even at last night's dinner party you vanished before midnight. Two, despite this newfound domesticity, you look like you've forgotten how to sleep. Circles beneath your eyes, sentences trailing off unfinished, a constant air of distraction. Three, you've had paint beneath your fingernails every day for a fortnight." The earl sat back in his chair, smugness rolling off him like mist. "It's plain as a pikestaff," he said. "You've found a muse."

John's breath escaped him in a rush of relief. A muse—but not a lover. "I can't tell you who she is."

The earl quirked one aristocratic eyebrow. "Because I wouldn't approve?"

"Because *she* wouldn't approve," John returned.

The earl chuckled. "And now I'm imagining you in thrall to some ancient duchess: imperious, dignified, and sharp of tongue."

John had a blinding vision of Hecuba at sixty, clad in violet, glaring at someone with that narrow-eyed gaze of hers and pursing her lips in suspicion. That bright hair threaded with gray, her skin papered with lines, each one a testament to the experience of some thought, some moment, some deed. He ached to think he'd never see her like that. "Maybe someday."

An elbow in his side broke into his thoughts. "But more likely it's someone a little more succulent, eh? Some luscious young tart pouting and preening while your cock all but punctures the canvas in front of you."

John pushed his plate away, his appetite abruptly gone. "It's not like that," he said, though he could feel a betraying flush warming his cheeks.

Simon shrugged this denial aside. "It must be convenient to have such a means of seduction available to you—the rest of us have to use shiny rocks and winning words to lure women into undressing. You just wave a paintbrush at them and the clothes vanish."

John ground his teeth together and managed not to respond. But he could feel a coldness creeping into his bones, washing away last night's glow. For a moment he even thought that he could hate Simon for this—but the thought burned out before it was more than half-lit and left only ash behind.

The earl stuck a piece of bacon in his mouth and chewed jauntily. "When will you show us the new paintings?"

"Why would I show them to you, of all people?" John retorted. "You've hated every brushstroke of every painting I've ever done. You've disagreed with every goal I have as an artist." He rose from the table with a barely controlled shove. "These are some of the best and most personal works I've ever done—why would I torture you with art you despise, and torture myself even worse by making room for your disdain?"

He ignored the flash of regret on Simon's face, and strode out of the room.

When he heard the front door open and shut a few minutes later, he knew his brother had left the house on some social errand or other. Relieved, John hurried up the stairs to the attic. The morning sunlight was rosy and warm, and John desperately hoped it might chase away the melancholy that shadowed him.

He prepared his pigments and removed his jacket, throwing a smock over his real clothes to forestall the wrath of Vickery. Then he dragged his easel closer to one of the windows, and set on it a canvas whose background was a swath of creased cream sheets and thick red curtains. It had always made him nervous to paint from memory rather than from life, but this time his brushstrokes were clear and confident. As though his hands knew what he needed even though his brain did not.

Slowly, Hecuba's form took shape in an attitude he recalled from the night before. She lay completely nude and lounging on her right side, languid and sated, eyes mostly but not entirely closed—just a hint of flutter on the lowered lids as though she were going to awake in the very next moment. Her skin was warm, flushed, her hair a tangle of paler golds and oranges than he'd used in *Circe* or for the water nymph.

John curled her left arm at her waist and stretched the other out in a graceful line, the portion near the shoulder pillowing her head, her hand hanging off the bed with fingers drowsily arched. *Aurora*, he would call it, after the goddess of rosy-fingered dawn. He'd always thought her friendlier than the other Olympians— more willing to take mortal lovers, more free to enjoy the physical pleasures they brought her. Not all her paramours had stories that ended happily, but she seemed to treat them with more warmth and affection than did Apollo or Venus or the perpetually callous Zeus.

At length he stood back and surveyed his own work. It was nearly finished, but not quite. The curve of Hecuba's hip, the length of her leg, the delicate expression on her face, these were all just as he pictured them. But something was missing...

His brush moved almost without conscious volition, gathering zinc white and just a hint of Indian yellow for contrast. A few strokes, a few shadows and there it was: his cravat, draped around her wrist, the linen's creased ends falling pale against the warmer color of the bedclothes.

There. The rightness of it, the solidity of that detail anchored the whole idea. The initial figure was a sleeping goddess, ethereal and untouchable, but that cravat was tied around the arm of a living, breathing woman of mortal flesh and blood. A woman bringing light and passion, a woman who lit him up like a bonfire.

This was no casual love affair for him, not anymore.

And this painting was the closest he'd come to an honest portrait in five years.

He'd always loved doing portraits but he'd stopped when his past efforts had been made the butt of family jokes and constant teasing. Little things, perhaps, no different than the much-repeated stories about his brother's school pranks or how his sister had learned to curse by eavesdropping on the stableboys. John's family, in short, treated his painting as something he would eventually outgrow and put aside as childish and frivolous. It seemed like a hobby to them, a quirk, rather than the calling John knew it to be.

This constant disregard had wormed its way beneath John's

skin and bitten deep. It had clumsied his fingers and filled his heart with a creeping, deathless anxiety. How dare he think he was creating anything like art? Wasn't it all just a vain and expensive form of self-gratification? Simon's insinuations about nude models and prurient painters had insulted him not because they were vulgar—though they certainly were—but because they assumed that he could have no motive other than sexual for being interested in painting people. In reality John was often transfixed by the way light fell on someone's hair or the angle at which another person held their head or the movement of hands or the moment right before someone smiled, when you could see it in their eyes but not yet in their mouth. There were entire gestural languages there to be deciphered—masters had tried for centuries past, and John yearned to be counted among their number.

How appalling it was to think he'd let whole years pass in quiet despair, a prisoner of fear and habit, when he could have been trying and failing and learning. His time was not endless, and he'd wasted quite enough of it.

He wanted painting in his life again.

And he wanted Hecuba Jones. All of her. He was more than willing to give all of himself in return—though he doubted the exchange was a fair one. She'd already given him more than he could ever hope to repay.

His eye wandered over to a painting leaning against the wall. It was the third C. F. Jones, he realized—Hecuba had forgotten to take it with her this morning in her rush to escape.

There was certainly no way he could take it to her now. They'd been formally introduced, certainly, but one did not go handing out expensive paintings to ladies one had only publicly talked to once. It would be a scandal, though probably not a ruinous one.

But, he realized with a grin, one could offer a lady a bouquet. Even a debutante. Even a debutante one had only just met.

With no time to waste, John began promptly to work.

It was afternoon and Hecuba was staring at the wallpaper. This was because the wallpaper, old and familiar though it was, was significantly more interesting than Mr. Bertram Egley, who was sitting beside Hecuba staring with puzzlement into his teacup.

"Do you think I've added enough lemon, Miss Jones?" he inquired.

How many lemons do idiots usually take in their tea? "I couldn't say," Hecuba replied.

"I'm just not sure one slice is enough," he went on, sniffing at the rapidly cooling surface of the tea. "But two may be too many and upset the balance of flavors."

Hecuba regretted the fact that lemons were the sharpest thing on the tea tray. "Mmm," she murmured, as uninterested a sound she could manage without being actually rude.

Mr. Egley's philosophical inquisition continued, unfortunately. "Some people might add sugar to counteract the acidity of the fruit, but I find that too much of that makes the beverage cloying and equally unappetizing." He sniffed again at the tea.

Hecuba drank from her own cup and wished it were deep enough to drown in.

On the other side of the room, Mr. Egley's elder brother Harold was smiling at Evangeline, whose eyes were lowered demurely. Hecuba knew her Aunt Pym hoped they would make a match of it, though tongues would wag if Evangeline was betrothed before her elder sister. Anne was sitting beside her mother, her eyes slightly glazed over, though her politely attentive expression remained perfectly starched and unspoiled.

Mr. Bertram Egley began to critique the crumpets.

Hecuba's knuckles went white as she folded her hands in her lap. Teatime visits were the bane of her existence. Hour upon hour of rote conversation, false smiles and tiny advances made toward mediocre ends. Hecuba would have nothing to show for her time at the end of the day. And yet the world expected her to flatter and please and ensnare some stiff-necked, stiff-brained gentleman just so this endless cycle of tedium could swallow all her remaining hours like the largest and laziest of monsters.

The sooner she was on her own, the better. She had half the paintings she needed and an arrangement that would gain her the others. Once she had collected all four, her real life could begin.

She had been in such a hurry this morning to leave Rushmore's house that she'd forgotten about the painting. But then she hadn't actually posed for a portrait last night, either—it was entirely possible that Rushmore would insist on lengthening the whole affair by at least another night so he might have the full four paintings he'd demanded. Hecuba allowed that an additional night with Rushmore was an enticing prospect. But it could go no further than that.

She allowed as well that her dread of their separation was getting stronger. She could feel its cold fingers wrapped around her beating heart, squeezing and stifling the strength of that muscle. To tear herself free of that grip would leave scars behind, scars that might never fully heal.

But much as she loathed the thought of the pain to come, Hecuba could not regret the choices she'd made that had led her to Rushmore's bed. He'd opened up her world in a very significant way. The physical pleasures had been illuminating, of course, but what she would miss most was the feeling that there were no masks or barriers between herself and another person. The sheer intimacy of sharing one's mind and—yes, she would admit it—one's heart with a passionate, intelligent partner, who could appreciate her opinions even if he didn't always agree.

Hecuba pulled her thoughts away from such a road lest they tempt her to weep— though she suspected that many before her had wept upon being forced into conversation with Mr. Bertram Egley. That gentleman was now mercifully silent and looking at the door, which was swinging open for the butler to announce and admit a new guest.

"The Honorable John Rushmore."

Hecuba's every muscle tightened in shock.

It was indeed Rushmore, decently clothed for once and grinning at her while Anne made the introductions to the other guests. Hecuba realized she'd never seen him in daylight before—but a more minute examination of the changes this made to his appearance would have to wait, as the gentleman had now pulled out from behind his back the most hideously large bouquet Hecuba had ever seen in her life. It looked like a small shrubbery, improbably studded with an overabundance of flowers, assembled apparently at random and with no regard for sense or symmetry.

"Dear Lord," Mr. Bertram Egley whispered in horror, "the *fuchsias*."

For the first time in all their acquaintance, Hecuba was inclined to agree with him. She pushed herself up from her chair as Rushmore approached, brandishing the floral monstrosity like the weapon it was.

"My dear Miss Jones," he said and now he was close enough for her to see the light of mischief in his eyes, "I have brought you something rather special."

He presented her with the monster, tilting it slightly forward so she was looking right down into the heart of the beast. She let her eyes roam in horror from the roses to the lilies to the inexplicable large-bladed leaves of grass—and that was when she noticed that all those eye-searing blooms had been woven around a thick, rolled core of canvas.

Her eyes darted back up to his and he nodded very slightly.

The madman had brought her the third painting hidden in plain sight. In that moment, Hecuba tumbled into love with John Rushmore.

It was the worst possible discovery at the worst possible time.

Everyone was watching; she had to say something. She dredged up a smile from some deep inner reserve and took the massive bouquet from Rushmore's hands. "Why thank you, Mr. Rushmore, for such an exuberant gift—and so impressively sized, too."

He nearly choked on a laugh and bowed to cover it. Mr. Egley coughed and Aunt Pym hastily cleared her throat. "Hecuba," she said, "please put Mr. Rushmore's bouquet somewhere...appropriate."

There was no appropriate place for something so ghastly inappropriate—gracious, were those *pine boughs* in there?—but Hecuba took advantage of the opportunity to get the painting into a safe place. Five minutes' quick work left leaves and petals scattered all over the coverlet on her bed, but she was able to unroll the painting at last.

The canvas was small, only a few handspans in width. What it depicted was *Artemisia*, Hecuba's mother's sly self-portrait as the famous female painter of centuries past. A slim, dark-haired woman in modern dress faced the viewer, palette and paintbrush in her hand. A nearby easel showed a perfect copy in miniature of *Judith Slaying Holofernes*—two women in antique robes holding down a bare-chested man, while the steelier-eyed of the two sawed at his neck with a sword. The arresting forms and vivid gore of the miniature were contrasted with the pale sunlight and peaceful scene of the dark-haired painter—yet her eyes, too, were steely as they looked back at the viewer, one corner of her mouth lifted at a joke known only to herself. The brushwork was restrained and meticulous, shadows created by the merest hint of a line, clear forms appearing out of minute suggestions of color.

It was impossible to say whether the picture's title referred to the dark-haired woman or to the fact that the painting within a painting was a copy of one of the historical Artemisia's most famous works. Cynthia Jones had died before her daughter had been able to ask the question.

Hecuba's fingers traced briefly over her mother's painted face, careful not to press too hard and crack the delicate surface. This was the only self-portrait C. F. Jones had ever allowed herself. Even there she had to hide within layers of history and veiled allusion, lest her identity be revealed to the embarrassment of her well-born family. Hecuba could only imagine the strength and dedication it had taken to keep working around and against such strictures. Her Aunt Pym had found it incomprehensible.

John Rushmore would have understood completely.

No wonder she loved him. But what on earth could she do about it?

Perhaps—it was the tiniest seedling of hope, but for the first time Hecuba allowed it to take root—perhaps he would understand her plans for her future as well. He couldn't be part of them, not officially, as where Hecuba was going no gentleman could follow without destroying his own social standing. But then they weren't really officially connected now, were they? Why shouldn't they preserve an affair that was so rewarding and pleasurable for them both? As long as it was kept a secret, they would have nothing to worry about.

Perhaps she didn't have to lose him after all.

The idea made her breathless, so she took a few moments to compose herself before heading back downstairs. When she returned to the parlor, she immediately noticed a new geography. Evangeline was still seated beside Harold Egley, but Bertram Egley was now being plied with cake by Aunt Pym while Rushmore lounged in Mr. Egley's abandoned seat.

Anne—a smiling, blushing Anne leaning forward with enthusiasm—had taken Hecuba's chair.

Hecuba could spot the hand of her matrimony-minded aunt in this. It was only natural that the social ivy should yearn to cling to the wealthy and well-featured younger brother of an earl. But did Anne have to look so very becoming in that particular shade of pink? And did she have to have so charming a laugh?

Jealously curled like a serpent in the belly. Hecuba narrowed her eyes.

Ignoring her Aunt Pym's meaningful glances, she strode over and sat on a sofa to Rushmore's left. He turned at once to face her, which Hecuba was forced to admit soothed the serpent's sting a little. "Your cousin was just telling me, Miss Jones, that you are in the habit of distilling your own pigments."

Hecuba had been mustering a tart something or other for Rushmore's benefit, but this simple statement set her off course.

Anne, behind Rushmore, grinned encouragingly. "She's taken over half of the conservatory," said her cousin, while Hecuba gaped. "Mother scolds her sometimes when the chemical smell leaks into other areas of the house."

"If she wouldn't keep closing the windows, she wouldn't have to worry so much," Hecuba retorted while Rushmore chuckled. "I made a batch of vermillion last week and it took hours for the fumes to dissipate. Closing the windows was more than a little dangerous—and it's not as though she does any gardening there herself."

"I should like to see these colors of yours sometime," Rushmore said. "You may not know it, Miss Jones, but I am something of a painter myself."

"Only something, Mr. Rushmore?" Hecuba shook her head in mock disapproval. "You will have to be a complete painter if you hope to impress me."

"Give me the right pigments, Miss Jones, and I promise I shall." He leaned forward, conspiracy on his lips and challenge in his eyes. "The vermillion, perhaps?"

Anne interrupted, leaping to her feet. "I know where it's kept —I'll fetch it." Her mother sent her a stern glance, intended no doubt to intimidate the girl back into her seat beside the eligible gentleman. Anne ignored this entirely and breezed from the room.

Aunt Pym's vengeance for this was swift and cruel: she sent Mr. Bertram Egley over with a cup of tea for Rushmore. "Lemon or cream, sir?" he inquired. "I'd recommend one slice of lemon, though it still isn't a perfect balance of flavors."

Rushmore thanked him and put two slices of lemon in his tea. "I've always appreciated a little extra tartness," he replied, smiling sidelong at Hecuba.

This man had seen and touched every inch of her, had caused her to curse and beg and berate him for who knows how many things—yet even a slantwise compliment from him could make her blush with pleasure. Oh, she was a sorry case indeed.

"Besides," Rushmore went on to the oblivious Egley, "you must know that the longer the tea steeps, the more robust the brew and the more lemon you can add without fear."

Mr. Egley's face lit up. "Of course, you are right!" he exclaimed and hurried back to where Aunt Pym was supervising Evangeline's pouring of the new pot of tea. Soon he returned with two more cups—one for himself and one for Hecuba, which he presented with a not-ungraceful flourish.

She took a sip just to be polite. Lemon and the barest hint of sugar twined around the richer flavors like cats around a well-loved ankle. It was easily the most delicious cup of anything she'd ever tasted in her life. She blinked in surprise. "Why, Mr. Egley, this is wonderful!"

He reddened and dropped his eyes. "I do so like to get these things right," he said. "Your cousin has an instinct for a well-brewed pot as well." With a slight bow, he crossed the room and took a seat beside Evangeline, who brightened visibly and began chatting with rather more than her usual animation.

His elder brother frowned before being distracted by Aunt Pym.

Hecuba took another sip of tea. Divine. "I should have more patience with Mr. Egley in future."

Rushmore considered the man, who had absorbed Evangeline in a debate on the merits of various cakes. "I'd like to get his opinion on port someday," he said. "A palate like his is a rare thing indeed."

"And yet you observed it after a minute's acquaintance," Hecuba said. "I've known the man for months and it never crossed my mind to take him seriously."

"Oh, he shouldn't be taken entirely seriously," Rushmore admitted. "But I like to think that everyone has some element of genius in them. The trick is to find it. Mr. Egley's was far more apparent than most."

Hecuba considered this for a long moment. "What's mine?"

His smile was full of awareness, the knowing look he usually wore in the nights they shared, and it took her breath away. "I can think of a few things you do *exceptionally* well," he teased, but then the glint in his eyes became a steadier light. "But I think the base and bedrock of your genius is this, Miss Jones—you have a great talent for remaking the world around you."

Hecuba snorted.

Rushmore ignored this. "It shouldn't surprise me to learn you're a colorist. There's more than a little alchemy in that, you know. Taking a substance, separating its elements, purifying them and recombining them to make something new and surprising."

He leaned forward, one hand coming to rest on the arm of the sofa. "When something isn't right in your eyes—when someone, for instance, has sold something that ought to have come to you— you do something to change it."

"That adventure did not go precisely as I planned," Hecuba pointed out, with a quick glance at Aunt Pym.

"No," Rushmore concurred, lowering his voice, "but you adapted your plans to suit the events that followed. You wanted those paintings back. You will get them—and you've transformed both my life and yours in the process."

"Two lives do not make up a world, Mr. Rushmore."

"They can, Miss Jones," he replied. His gloved hand brushed her shoulder—a touch invisible but not unfelt.

At that moment, Anne returned with a stoppered vial in her hand. She presented it to Rushmore then threw herself on her proverbial sword by taking an empty seat beside her mother. Aunt Pym immediately directed her attention to Harold Egley, apparently giving Evangeline up as a lost matrimonial cause, at least for the present.

Rushmore was holding the vermillion in the light, turning it around to watch the fine red grains tumble against the surface of the glass. "This is quite a pure hue, Miss Jones," he said. "May I keep it?"

"So long as you do not keep it for long," Hecuba said with a mischievous smile of her own. "It was made to be used, not simply bottled up and admired."

He grinned and tucked the vermillion into a pocket. "There is a particular vision I should like to attempt—say, in two nights' time."

"Two nights," Hecuba agreed softly. The assignation thus arranged and with her relatives none the wiser, she smiled demurely into her teacup.

CHAPTER 9

*T*he next morning John slept quite late and spent his afternoon buying more canvas and supplies. He was going through them at a rather alarming rate—not even his generous funds would support this forever—but he felt as though he were making up for years of lost time. He could afford to be temperate in his old age rather than in the prime working years of his artistic life.

With that in mind, he stopped in at his club for supper before heading home.

The whole house was ablaze when he returned—odd, since Simon hadn't mentioned any social engagements to him. But indeed there was the clink of plates, the faint odor of a feast recently devoured, and the oceanic murmur of a dinner party on its third glass of wine. Baritone and bass voices swelled like the tides, while the altos and sopranos shimmered above them like foam.

The earl met him in the hallway, glass of champagne in hand. "Where have you been?" he demanded, but just as quickly waved the question aside. "No matter. Evening clothes—now."

John's answer was a ludicrously deep bow with several

elaborate curls of his hand. Simon snorted and returned to his guests.

Vickery had already laid out the proper attire. John handed over the parcel of painting supplies and began unbuttoning. "Shall I take these up to the north attic, sir?" the valet inquired.

John's hands paused mid-button. "The north attic?"

"That is where you've been painting, sir, is it not?"

Unease bubbled up from the depths. "Yes it is," he admitted. "But you can leave them here—I'll take them up myself."

"Very good, sir." Vickery helped John into his coat and approved the knot of his cravat. John's anxiety trailed him like a ghost as he descended the stairs to the card room, where the party seemed to be centered.

Simon met him at the foot of the stairs and handed him a glass of champagne. "For the nerves," he said enigmatically.

John could only stare at him. "What is all this?" he asked. It was not the most eloquent of responses but it had the benefit of being to the point.

Simon tapped his nose with a finger. "A surprise," was all he would say.

John downed the champagne in a single draught.

The voices ebbed as he entered the room then surged again to an even higher pitch. He recognized almost everyone present as part of the fast Bohemian set: school friends turned rakehells, poetic types, sloe-eyed widows, and known eccentrics. One ancient and regal woman in a turquoise turban winked at him. There were no blushing debutantes, no stolid, red-faced landholders, no withered members of parliament or ice-eyed social patronesses in sight.

And by now nearly everyone had turned to look at him. John felt the hairs on the back of his neck lift. "Simon?" he murmured again.

"It's all right," his brother said. "I just wanted to show you that the family is proud of you."

"Proud?" John asked. His brain felt as though it were rusted over, the wheels and cogs unable to turn and complete the process of comprehension.

"As a painter," Simon said patiently.

And then John saw them.

His canvases and sketches, all of them, ranged around the room in pools of candlelight. Everywhere Hecuba's half-captured form, painted and posed and displayed in all its evident glory. In pride of place were the three large oils—*Circe, Hylas and the Naïad* and—oh God, no—*Aurora.*

The pose that had seemed so intimate and worshipful when he'd painted it became lurid and debauched in the presence of so many avid onlookers. The red background, the tumbled sheets and most of all that obscenely tied cravat that brought a male, modern presence into the painting and charged it with sexual immediacy.

From the flames that surrounded her, Hecuba smiled.

John looked wildly around but it was clear from the knowing looks and behind- hand whispers that at least one guest had recognized the model. Word was spreading. The scandal had its wings already.

John rushed out of a side door to the garden and retched into a bush. He kept heaving long after his stomach was empty, sliding down to his knees with his hands on the wrought-iron railing, breathing in great gulps of cold night air.

Simon's hand came down on his shoulder and a glass of water appeared. John ignored it, despite the burning in his throat that made it hard to force the words out. "You. Have ruined. *Everything.*"

"Oh, get up," Simon said, patting his shoulder. John shook him off but rose to his feet, hands clenching and unclenching restlessly. His brother continued, "I know it's a bit of a shock, but now no one can deny your talent as an artist. And your model has quite a promising start as a professional beauty." He threw out a suggestive elbow. "No wonder you've been keeping her to yourself—she's a staggering creature! Though there is something familiar in the face...Did you find her at the opera? Covent Garden?" John could only sputter on hearing that, which only made Simon's grin wider. "Somewhere even less reputable?"

That was Simon—the elder brother, the heir, always so smug, always so *right*. In a flash John had him up against the wall, hands fisted in Simon's lapels, choking the superior breath right out of him. "Do you recall," John managed, though it was hard to unclamp his jaw against the fury, "two weeks ago when we went to Lord Heatherton's ball?"

Simon fought against his brother's grip but was too shocked to succeed. "Let go!" he choked.

"We met the ladies of a charming family, rather new to London," John ground out.

Simon froze. John watched the moment of realization pass like a shroud over his face, paling everything beneath. "The sisters..." he breathed. "The cousin with the red hair."

"Miss Hecuba Jones," John confirmed. He gave Simon one more small throttle for good measure, then released him and stepped away. "A lady—not an opera singer and not a whore. I won't claim we've behaved with all due propriety, but we were managing just fine between us." He scrubbed at his mouth, bitterness all he could taste. "Until tonight."

Simon brushed his hands down the front of his coat, smoothing away the wrinkles. He narrowed his eyes. "Next you'll be telling me you didn't fuck her, though you obviously spent a great deal of painting time staring at her tits."

John's pulse spiked high with a rage so sudden that it dizzied him. "That's none of your damn business."

"So you *have* fucked her."

"I was hoping to marry her!" John shouted, bringing Simon up short.

"That's good to hear, dear brother," he said after a moment, "because that's exactly what you're going to do."

John's night, from that point, proceeded to get even worse.

His brother ended the party abruptly and sent the guests

away. John chafed at the thought that this would only give more speed to the rumors, but the thought of trying to smile his way through the rest of the night was intolerable. The last candle in the card room had barely been extinguished before Simon was ordering the carriage and demanding that John tell him where Hecuba lived. "It's always better to confront the problem head-on," was all the earl would say.

John fought the urge to wipe that arch expression right off Simon's face with a well-thrown right to the jaw. "There is no way in hell you are coming with me," he growled.

Simon sent him the exact same glare their father had used, back when the worst trouble his sons caused had been to switch the salt and sugar in the kitchen. "This was my mistake," Simon said, "even though you laid the foundations. I refuse to relinquish my share of the consequences. The family must preserve some honor."

John turned his face away and let the argument die. He was already twisted and breaking inside at the thought of what he had to tell Hecuba. Of her image, splayed out for the titillation of his brother's guests. Of what the news would do to her and their fragile, hard-won trust.

He thought of telling her that she had no choice but to marry him and knew at once that she was going to refuse.

Rage was doused and turned to ash by the sickening awareness that he'd lost everything important in his life.

Oh, he would recover from the scandal eventually. The gentleman always did in cases like these. There would be a few high-placed sticklers who would write him off as a lost cause, but far and away the majority would gasp and giggle and forget all about it over the course of a few quietly lived years.

Hecuba, however, was irrevocably ruined. Painted in the nude then displayed for all his friends to gawk at! It was beyond shocking. It would destroy her whole family.

God, he hadn't even had a chance to tell her about the third painting! He'd presumed so much. He'd believed he could keep a secret by sheer willpower. He'd borrowed her likeness without her knowledge and used it as a weapon against her. How could he ever paint again after this?

How could he paint without Hecuba?

How could he live without her?

How was he going to tell her about all this?

The Pyms' windows were dark and the household abed when they arrived, but it did not remain so for long. The family gathered in the parlor, rubbing the sleep from their eyes and smoothing their hands over hair disordered by blankets and pillows. John's palms were clammy and his knees shaky. He locked them in place, looked directly at Hecuba and forced himself to begin the story.

He explained, for the benefit of her aunt and uncle, that they'd had an arrangement to trade her mother's paintings for the new ones he would paint with Hecuba as a model. He left out her attempted theft and especially their mutual seduction, because if he had to profane that mystery as well he would be sick all over again. Hecuba narrowed her eyes at his obvious omissions, but allowed them to stand.

However, he was now at the difficult part.

"I painted a third painting," he said, twisting his hands behind his back. "Yesterday morning, without Hec—Miss Jones. No malice was intended, but I'm afraid I let myself get carried away. I...I painted something that I shouldn't have."

"What was that?" Hecuba's uncle demanded.

John flicked him a glance but the bulk of his attention remained on Hecuba herself. "A nude."

Aunt Pym shrieked and sank to the floor. Anne and Evangeline ran to help her, though they looked shocked and shaken themselves.

Hecuba only folded her arms. "And?" she said.

"What do you mean, 'And'?" her uncle spluttered.

"I want to know what happened between yesterday morning and the present late hour," Hecuba went on. "He didn't rush over to apologize for the painting then—what makes an apology necessary now?" Her face was serene, but there was a curious thickness in her voice. John ached to wrap his arms around her and tell her everything would be all right, but he knew it wouldn't be—and he couldn't touch her until he'd told her the full story.

John allowed himself one deep breath. "Tonight, as a surprise, my brother invited a number of people he thought would appreciate the new paintings he'd found I'd been making. He was trying to show me he was proud of my work." The word *proud* slithered off his tongue, bitter as poison.

Uncle Pym let out an oath that degraded several generations of the Rushmore family. Simon, to his credit, never flinched. "And this vile painting—you exhibited it? In public?" Uncle Pym demanded.

"We showed all of them," John admitted, the sentence falling like a stone into the stillness of his audience. "All three paintings, plus a number of sketches and studies. All of Miss Jones." His breath rattled a little in his throat under the weight of the next bit. "Someone recognized her."

Aunt Pym let out a wail.

Hecuba's lips thinned and she closed her eyes.

John didn't feel any better now that the truth was out. "I'm sorry," he said. "So terribly sorry."

"Sorry?" yelled Uncle Pym. He took a great step forward and planted a fist in John's face. John let the blow fall without resistance, let it rock him back until he staggered up against the wall. His eye throbbed and pulsed and he knew it would be fully black by morning.

He still didn't feel any better. Hecuba hadn't yet opened her eyes.

Simon decided this was his opportunity. "Of course," he said to Uncle Pym, "my brother will marry your niece as soon as possible."

Just like that all the color began to leach out of the world.

Anything John could say now was tainted. He could shout that he loved Hecuba, that he had wanted to marry her anyway, that he only hoped she would accept an idiot like him as a spouse—and all they would hear was the shiny sound of a good boy doing his duty and following his brother's orders. "Miss Jones," he said, "would you allow me a few moments in private?"

Hecuba opened her eyes and oh, they were so cold. John had never seen eyes that cold in all his life. "No," she said.

"Hecuba, you must accept the gentleman—" said Aunt Pym.

"I will not." She said this calmly enough but it threw the rest of the family into an absolute uproar. Evangeline began to cry, Anne began to argue and Aunt Pym began another impossibly sustained howl of grief. Hecuba looked at John with the barest hint of pity in her expression. "I'm terribly sorry, Mr. Rushmore."

He'd known what she would say, yet still John's heart broke under those quiet words as though they weighed as much as mountains. If he opened his mouth the sounds would be inhuman, garbled noises of anguish, so instead of speaking he bowed to indicate his understanding.

"I could marry her myself," Simon offered, still addressing Uncle Pym. "People would be much less likely to speak out openly against a duchess, no matter how she came to the title."

John had only begun to comprehend the magnitude of his horror at this suggestion when Hecuba spoke. "I appreciate your strategy, my lord, but I refuse your offer as well." John let out a breath he didn't realize he'd been holding, and slumped harder against the wall. "I have other plans for my future," Hecuba continued. "They do not include marriage—not even to save myself from scandal."

John's last feeble spark of hope winked out like a candle dropped into the sea. Aunt Pym's wailing climbed several steps in pitch.

"What plans?" Uncle Pym demanded.

"I'm going to be a colorman," said Hecuba. "Or woman as it were."

Even Aunt Pym went silent, at least for long enough to take an uneven breath. "You're going into trade?" she whispered with a shudder.

"I am going to make and sell pigments," Hecuba confirmed. "Mother always said I had a talent for it, and she was right. I have been practicing for some time now and feel confident in my skills. It will only take a very little money to get me started—supplies and a space to work in."

"And where are these funds going to come from?" her uncle sneered. Hecuba pressed her lips together and maintained a stony silence.

"Shameless trollop," gasped Aunt Pym.

Uncle Pym's brow furrowed. He gripped his wife's shoulder and glared at his niece. "You take too much after your mother. I am ashamed to have treated you like a proper member of this family. You will gather your things in the morning and be gone—I won't permit you to spend one more night beneath my roof."

Anne leapt to her feet and her cousin's defense. "This roof was rented with money *he* gave you," she said, pointing to John, "for paintings you had no right to sell! And now you *dare* to cast her out, when you are the cause of all these troubles in the first place?"

"Which of my daughters told me the thing they wanted most in the world was a Season and a good match?" Uncle Pym replied in clipped tones. Anne cried out in protest but her father remained adamant. "If we do not show our disapproval swiftly and decisively, your prospects and your sister's will be sacrificed to your cousin's feeble moral judgment."

Anne strode over to stand beside her cousin. Hecuba looked far more surprised by that than she had by John's initial revelation. "Society can be cruel," said Anne, "but it would be crueler of us to treat its rules as gospel." She wound her hand around Hecuba's and raised her chin. "If you throw her out, I'm going with her."

Uncle Pym sputtered but found no words to counter his

daughter's ultimatum. Hecuba smiled something very like a real smile.

John's heart lifted to see it, hopeless though he was. They made quite the pair: Anne dark and defiant, Hecuba shaken but stoic. His mind was halfway done with the initial sketch before he shook the dream away.

The earl turned to John with a scowl. "Aren't you going to say *anything*?" Simon demanded.

Six pairs of eyes fastened themselves on John. It seemed the very world was holding its breath, giving him a chance to make some stirring proclamation, pull a white horse out of his sleeve, throw Hecuba over his shoulder and ride away in search of the nearest clergyman. Or Scotland. Aunt Pym would tell her friends how romantic it had been. Uncle Pym would grouse into his claret about young men's impulses but give the rascal credit for doing his duty. Simon would consider it a fit punishment for his lack of gentlemanly behavior, and would no doubt find himself rather fond of Hecuba, once he got to know her. As for the presumed bride herself...

Hecuba's face threatened cold vengeance if he tried anything of the kind.

Her decision meant there was no decision for him to make. It was curiously liberating, though the relief echoed hollowly within him. "No," he said to the unimportant everyone. "I have nothing else to say. I will honor our agreement and send your niece the last of her mother's paintings." He bowed to Hecuba, who inclined her head in return. "Miss Jones, if you should ever need anything, all you have to do is ask." Then, ignoring the storm of curses, shouts and horrified gasps, John turned on his heel and strode from the room.

When word of the scandal spread, the Pym family was cut off like a gangrenous limb. Absent the constant round of visiting and visitors, the world seemed very quiet. Hecuba told herself this was for the best, and spent as much time as possible in the conservatory, away from her aunt's dramatic sobs and her uncle's icy silences.

But she couldn't avoid them forever. Dining together became an impossible ordeal. She didn't know which was worse: Evangeline's near-constant weeping or Aunt Pym's vicious comments. Night after night Hecuba was treated to a catalog of all the ways she'd failed as a niece, as a lady and as a Christian. Even Anne, who had initially tried to rebuff these attacks, was soon reduced to simmering silently and waiting for her aunt's eloquence to flag.

Hecuba bit her tongue until it bled and resolved to leave the house as soon as possible. Her cousins' situation would improve once she was gone—if it weren't for her guilt over how Anne and Evangeline were suffering, she could have laughingly shaken free of all her aunt's venom. It couldn't even come close to wounding her as much as John Rushmore had.

One week later, the butler informed her that several parcels had arrived addressed to her. "From the Earl of Underwood," he said, pitching his voice low.

Hecuba instructed him to take them upstairs at once.

Safe in her bedroom, with shaking hands, Hecuba opened the first parcel.

Three figures lounged in a fire-lit room. A brown-haired gentleman sat with his feet up, smoking a pipe, looking fondly at a dark-haired woman. This lady had a book in one hand, but was not reading from it. Instead, smiling, she was combing gentle fingers through the bright red hair of a little girl whose knees were on the floor but whose head was pillowed in her mother's lap. Of course it was Hecuba, her mother and father. *A Winter Evening*, it was called, and the spaces outside the family circle were chill with snow and bristling with greenery.

A second parcel turned out to be herself, nude, with a cravat tied around her wrist. Hecuba's throat ached at the happiness reflected in her painted features. She remembered the slide of linen against her skin, the tension of restraint, the feel of Rushmore's body plunging into hers. She remembered how he'd laughed at her irritation and soothed her worries. She remembered how agony had sliced through her when she'd learned of this painting's existence—knives were ticklish in comparison. She'd imagined something lurid and ridiculous, or something too idealized and worshipful and therefore silly in the eyes of onlookers. But this was warm, sweet, and human while still being beautiful and sensual. This was how Rushmore had made her feel.

Her whole self ached with missing him.

When she went to open the third and final parcel, she noticed that a letter had been attached.

My dear Jones,

I wish very much that I had the right to tell you all that I'm feeling. But my feelings are not your obligations. Since you wish to end it, all that remains is this: I wish it had ended differently. So wondrous a beginning deserved a better coda, if it had to end.

Please accept not only the remaining painting of your mother's, as promised, but also your own portraits, including the fourth and final one. They are yours to do with as you please. At first I thought of keeping them, I admit, but it made me feel like some mad alchemist of ages past, surrounding himself with lead in the hope that it might someday turn into gold. But that's your specialty, not mine.

The new painting is called Thief of Hearts. *Yours,*

John

Hecuba pulled away the concealing paper.

It was a dark canvas, nearly black, with hints of deep green and a few splashes of vermillion that she recognized as her own concoction. Moonlight flowed in from the picture's left, outlining a tall window and a figure in the process of leaping over the sill— a woman in black with red hair bound tightly back from a pale and mischievous profile. A necklace of heart-shaped rubies as bright as fire swung from one hand as she held open the window sash with the other. The edges of the figure were blurred, as if caught in the middle of motion, so quick and elusive that the eye itself was barely fast enough to catch her.

But oh, it was the shadows that broke her heart.

As with *Circe*, the margins of this painting were inhabited. But instead of tortured bodies and grasping hands, the figures here were plain, dark, and unvaryingly forlorn. Hooded and ghostly, they inclined toward the fleeing thief like headstones in an ancient graveyard, night-black robes swirling down around their ankles. Each one pressed a hand to its cloaked breast, as though in mourning for a heart that beat there no longer.

It was the loneliest image Hecuba had ever seen.

He was letting her go.

The thought made her breathless, grateful and mournful all at once. He had accepted her rejection as final without berating her, without belittling her and without bullying. Her family was not willing to allow her the luxury of refusal, but Rushmore offered it as a matter of course.

She loved him so very much.

She leaned *Thief of Hearts* against the wall beside *A Winter Evening*. The two paintings complemented each other perfectly— reds and blacks, whites and greens, motion and peace, light and shadow. They belonged together, one on either side of the mantel. Depending on how you arranged them, the thief could either be leaping toward or running away from the family and their cozy fireplace.

Hecuba had placed her leaping toward.

She sighed. That was telling. It was not the mystical properties or prophetic nature of oil paint that spoke to her, but the realization that she was looking for reasons to change her mind.

It was galling to think that she felt the need for reasons. Rushmore hadn't asked for hers when she'd refused his proposal. Her refusal had been reason enough—and none of the pressures their families brought to bear had been able to change his mind.

He'd been strong enough to give her up merely because she'd asked.

Would he be strong enough to give up his way of life, if she offered herself in exchange?

Perhaps not. Perhaps he'd found it easier to let her go than to lose his comfortable existence and the pleasures of aristocratic society. It was a daunting thought. But Hecuba Jones had never yet backed down from a challenge.

It was time to tell Rushmore everything.

How strange to go through the unfamiliar front door and find herself in a very familiar room. How strange to feel her skirts tangling around her ankles and her stays hampering the easy in and out of her breathing. "What?" said Rushmore's voice when she knocked.

She opened the door to the earl's study, pulling in as much breath as she could against the rushed beat of her heart. A servant walked behind holding four rolls of canvas.

Rushmore slouched in the armchair on the hearth, legs stretched out on the ottoman. One hand was gripping a pencil, the other a glass of whisky. Neither hand had moved in quite some time, it seemed—the whisky glass was full and the page beneath the pencil was barren and blank.

His eyes widened when they fell on Hecuba but he said nothing.

Hecuba relieved the servant of his burden and dismissed him with a simple "Thank you."

She turned back to Rushmore, arms wrapped around the bulk of canvas, trying to untie her tongue. His coat was tossed negligently on the chair beside him, his waistcoat hanging open and unbuttoned. He looked a ruin. "You haven't shaved," she said.

He shrugged. "I haven't cared to." He raised the glass of

whisky and toasted her with it. "Even getting drunk was too much work—I doubt I've had more than two sips from this, and I've been sitting here since noon."

"May I?" Hecuba put the canvas rolls aside and took the drink. She downed half the spirits in a single swallow and returned the glass to him, catching her breath a little when his fingers brushed hers.

"Feeling in want of courage, Jones?" he asked, one corner of his mouth lifting briefly, though his shoulders remained stiff and his eyes wary.

"Somewhat," Hecuba replied. "It isn't every day I propose to a gentleman."

Rushmore choked on his drink, whisky perfuming the air between them. He set the glass aside and put his feet on the floor, giving her his full attention. "Maybe I'm drunk after all," he said. "Are you really planning to propose? To me?"

"To you," she confirmed. "But you are allowed to refuse if you wish."

He held himself very still. Hecuba felt the distance between them like a gap in her own flesh. "Why the change of heart?"

"Not heart," she said. "Merely a change of circumstances."

He blinked, and waited.

She gathered her strength and began. "Here, at this moment, there are no hysterical aunts, no sympathetic cousins, no upright brothers to tell us what to choose. If I'd accepted you the other day, we would have married to prevent the worst thing from happening. There would have been a pall over the whole business right from the very start. If I were to change my mind about marriage, Rushmore, then I could only do so for the best reason. None of those reasons were good, let alone best. But now the worst has already happened and we have survived it. We are free."

He was unconvinced. "You think being ruined is the worst possible thing?"

"I think making a choice for the wrong reasons is the worst

possible thing. I think choosing other people's comfort over my own needs is the worst possible thing." She realized her hands were fidgeting and made them keep still. "I refused you not because of yourself, but because no one else in that room would have believed I'd said yes because I wanted to marry you." She sighed. "It is equally possible that stubbornness is my most overriding flaw, and I dislike being dictated to."

"I know that," he said, his voice as soft as firelight. "I know you, Jones."

"Oh," said Hecuba. Fluttering hope awoke and stretched its wings. "Then you probably already know as well that I love you."

Statues were less still than Rushmore was at present. "No, Jones," he whispered. "I had no idea."

"Well. I do love you. With all my heart." She took a deep breath. "I would be very honored, Rushmore, if you—"

She never had a chance to finish the sentence. Rushmore had finally shaken off his stillness and had yanked her into the chair with him. She fell in a froth of petticoats, gasping against his mouth as he kissed her with enough fire to combust what remained of the glass of whisky. She tried to move closer, to straddle his hips, but her skirts were too cumbrous, pinned beneath her knees and snagged on the heel of her shoe. His hands struggled alongside hers until he gave up, lifted her bodily and sent them both to the floor in a controlled hurtle.

From there it was easier—her skirts rose beneath his hands while she tugged at his hair and begged him to hurry. His rough fingers found the heat of her and plunged inside, teasing her with sweet thrusts. She pulled open his shirt and spread her legs, arching up to rub against the hard cock she could feel beneath his trousers. "Marry me," she said, pressing her mouth to the side of his neck. "Please."

He groaned, wrestled with his trousers and plunged his cock into her. Her gasp was ragged at the edges—if it felt any better, she would die here and now with a smile on her face. He fucked her hard, desperately, a horde of keening sounds falling from his throat. One of his hands plunged between them and unerringly he found her clitoris, stroking fast and hard. Hecuba bit his neck to keep from crying out as she came, clenching and shuddering around him, tightening deliciously around his plunging cock. He held himself deep and gasped aloud his own climax, shaking and throbbing and pouring himself into her.

"If that is how you say yes," Hecuba sighed, "then I shall propose every day until the wedding."

Rushmore rolled to the side with a laugh. "That is one way to say yes," he replied. "Here is another." His hand grazed her cheek as he smiled. "I love you, Hecuba Jones. I love you more than words. I love you more than life. I love you more than painting, if you can believe it."

Hecuba laughed, rose to one elbow and kissed him. "That reminds me. Perhaps you should not say yes until you know precisely what you are getting into."

"I'm getting into trade, aren't I? You're not giving up the idea of being a colorman just because you're marrying me, are you?"

"Does that bother you?"

"It certainly does," he said. "It bothers me very much if you give up so good a plan for so paltry a reason."

She smiled, but this was important. "It might make things very difficult for you."

He shrugged—as much as one can while lying on one's back. "My family won't disown me if that's what you're worried about. We're a small group—just my brother, my sister and the aunt she's travelling with in Italy. I won't miss the social whirl, either, especially as I intend to be very busy with my own work. Besides," Rushmore went on archly, "if my wife is a colorist, I expect to get a discount on paints."

"Help fund this enterprise and you can have all the paints you ever need," Hecuba said. "But I really ought to tell you where the other funds are coming from." She pushed herself to her feet, shook out her skirts and began unrolling the four paintings she'd brought with her. Amiably, Rushmore buttoned himself up and joined in. Soon all four C. F. Jones canvases were spread out along the desk. "Can you give us more light?" Hecuba asked.

Rushmore lit a taper and set it on the edge of the desk. By this time, Hecuba had aligned four of the paintings' corners so they met in a cross in the middle.

Rushmore sucked in a breath and leaned closer. "How...?" he asked. The brushstrokes that had seemed mere abstract filler when the paintings were separate were now revealed to form shapes together—a blue circle here, a winding brown snake, gray-green squares and at one point a bright, vivid X. Made of Hecuba green.

"It's a map," he breathed.

"The paintings are my mother's bequest," Hecuba explained. "I was to receive them when I came of age at twenty-one, along with her recipe book, including the formula for Hecuba green. And my father was a thief who was never caught—he had a small store of jewels when I was younger, some pearls and other stones he used to let me play with. None of those turned up when he died, either." She pointed at that blob of Hecuba green. "It's all waiting right there," she said. "I needed all four paintings to reconstruct the map."

Rushmore leaned on his hands. "You mean I've had a treasure map this whole time and never knew it?" He groaned. "Simon is never going to let me live this down."

"Simon never has to know," Hecuba replied tartly.

"Let's not tell him then," Rushmore agreed. He pulled Hecuba tight against him— not that she was resisting. She sighed and breathed in the warm, faintly earthy scent of him. "Shall we get married tomorrow?"

"So soon?" Hecuba answered. "I was hoping you'd say yes a few more times first."

Rushmore's eyes danced as he said, "Jones, I promise you—I'll say yes every day for the rest of my life."

~

"Is that it?" Rushmore asked, squinting beneath the cover of his hand.

"No, you idiot," Hecuba replied. "To the *east* of the pond. That's left."

"Left, east—who can tell in all these trees? Good thing I brought you along, wife," he said. "A treasure map is no good if you can't understand where it's telling you to go."

Hecuba muttered something about telling him *precisely* where to go, which only made him laugh. In truth, she was only irked by the blisters on her feet and the scratches on her arms. They were out in the country, two miles north of Hecuba's home parish, and certain paths had become much harder to navigate since her father first traversed them so many years before. The harder she cursed, the more amused Rushmore became. He knew she enjoyed a certain amount of grumpiness.

If she hadn't already married him the week before, she'd marry him again.

They found the right tree, an ancient oak keeping court over a circle of young and lovely birches. Rushmore pulled out the spade they'd brought with them and began to dig.

And dig.

And dig some more.

Just when Hecuba was thinking of *possibly* suggesting that *maybe* she'd been wrong, the spade went *thunk*. Rushmore's dirt-streaked, sun-reddened face broke into a grin.

A few more minutes work and they had between them a small iron box, thoroughly corroded. The shovel's blade was sturdy enough to break the old lock off the front, and Rushmore sat back on his heels. "Would my lady care to have the honors?"

Hecuba knelt, heedless of stains on her skirt or the damage to her stockings. The box's lid opened on the second try to reveal a fold of weathered black cotton.

Both Hecuba and Rushmore held their breath.

Her hands peeled back the cloth to reveal two small gold

bracelets, an enamel brooch and a pendant with a stone that might or might not have been an emerald.

Rushmore dropped the spade, which bit angrily into the earth. "That's it?" he asked.

"He must have sold the others while I was growing up," Hecuba said. "I half expected that. We never had much money—every penny would have been welcome."

"Well," Rushmore grumbled, then sighed. "That isn't the most important part of the treasure anyway ."

"No, it's not." Trust an artist to think of color as treasure. Hecuba smiled and pulled out the cloth, revealing a rough nailhead on the bottom of the metal box. She pressed on it, and on the outside of the box a small drawer snicked open. There were no jewels there at all, not even tawdry ones. Instead there was a slim black notebook carefully wrapped in oilcloth.

With reverent fingers, she turned to the first page. "Umber," she read and flipped a bit farther. "Chrome orange. Lead white. And—yes, here it is..." She presented one page to Rushmore with an air of triumph. "Hecuba green."

Her husband gave a whoop and threw his arms in the air. "You said the recipe had been lost!"

"It had been," Hecuba laughed. "Mother knew it by heart and I'd learned many of the rest—at least the ones we could make with limited equipment—but not all of them. There are some quite good ones in here as well as the green."

"Hecuba, my dear," Rushmore grinned, "we're going to be rich."

"Rushmore, my love," she retorted, "we already are."

NEXT: AT HIS COUNTESS' PLEASURE

The follow-up to A Thief in the Nude*! A decisive countess, a stalwart earl, a painful secret, and some light femdom. Get updates when you sign up for my newsletter, and I hope you enjoy this taste of what's ahead.*

Miss Anne Pym kept her eyes fixed on Rushmore House as she stepped out of the carriage. The building in front of her was white marble, gleaming in the winter sunlight like an ancient matriarch. Amazing how time could be so kind to a building, yet so unkind to a gown—Anne's pale pink muslin had seen only three years to compare to the great house's three decades, but where Rushmore House had silvered over with dignity, the gown had only faded and aged. Nevertheless, Anne strode bravely up the walkway while her maid Dorothy fluttered behind her like an errant handkerchief.

The butler who answered Anne's knock raised an eyebrow at her appearance, but admitted her and offered to show her to the parlor to wait.

"No, thank you," said the lady, "I shall see the earl at once, please."

Gently but firmly, the butler denied her.

Anne swept by him and ascended the stairs. The butler

abandoned the maid in the foyer and followed Anne, pleading in increasingly strident tones.

Her feet never faltered.

Though she had only been here twice before, Anne knew the way to the study. The door was open, so she sailed over the threshold without a pause and curtsied with all propriety to the man seated there.

Simon Rushmore, Earl of Underwood, rose from his desk and waved his butler into silence. "Thank you, Phillips," he said, not without sympathy. "Would you have Cook send up some tea for our guest?"

"No tea, thank you," said Anne.

The earl nodded acquiescence. Phillips bowed, spots of red staining his decorous cheeks, and the door closed whisper-soft behind him.

The earl tilted his head at Anne, clearly bemused. "To what do I owe the honor, Miss Pym?"

Anne had prepared herself for precisely this moment. She folded her hands in front of her and said, "I have come, my lord, for restitution."

The earl's eyebrows lifted.

Anne didn't wait for him to ask her to explain further. "Your brother did a great injury to my family when he seduced my cousin Hecuba and painted her...*en deshabille*," she said.

The earl sighed, not as though he'd forgotten the incident, but as though it weighed heavily on him. "He did indeed, Miss Pym, but they are married now. Surely honor has been satisfied?"

Anne had anticipated this denial and was determined to challenge it. "Your honor may be, but ours is still tarnished. John and Hecuba only married after the scandal had run its course. There was a full month of the Season when we were all quite thoroughly shunned—left isolated, disgraced, and avoided by anyone of name." And now that Hecuba had opened her shop and was selling paints to artists all over Britain, last year's scandal had new life on the lips of society's gossips this spring. *A cousin in trade! Can you credit it? Who would invite her anywhere, if not to gawk?* Anne realized her hands were twisting nervously together and set them into fists instead. "My cousin's marriage to your brother may have made them both deliriously happy, but it has done nothing to restore my family's social standing."

The earl grimaced, but he nodded. Quite as though she'd said something ordinary and reasonable. Anne allowed a small seed of hope to begin sprouting. "What do you suggest I do about it?" he asked. One corner of his mouth quirked up. "I assume you came here with a practical scheme in mind."

She had, and she was frank enough to admit it. "It's nothing so terrible. All I ask is that you host a few dinners, maybe a party or two, and invite us as well as your usual circle. My younger sister is pretty and charming and perfectly capable of attaching some eligible gentleman. She had a few excellent prospects last Season —I'm sure it would not take long for one of those sparks to rekindle. If she were given the opportunity."

His eyes were cool and considering. "And what of yourself, Miss Pym?"

The question hit a sore spot, pressing her lips into a thin line. Anne was realistic about her own capacity to allure. She had excellent posture and straight teeth and no noticeable blemishes on her skin, but no artist would ever beg to paint her portrait. She had eyes that could see well enough and a mouth that could form words and a nose that perched on her face as it was supposed to. As much as she had once wished otherwise, Anne Pym was as plain and serviceable as the brown woolen gowns she'd left behind her in the countryside.

She knew what she was. But more importantly, she knew what she wanted.

"I want a family," Anne said. "I want a husband who is kindhearted and who gives me at least three children. I want to have money enough to keep fed and warm in the winter, and not to have to worry about how to pay the cook's wages or buy new clothes for the children when they outgrow the old. I know something about money worries, my lord. My father has just enough funds left to give us one more Season in town, and I mean to make the most of it. It's possible there are men I knew in the country with whom I could be happy, but I would prefer to spread as wide a net as possible, the better to increase the odds." She caught her breath, having admitted more than she'd intended. It was hard not to when he was looking at her with such thoughtfulness. As if he were really listening. As if what she was saying were important. She was unused to the weight of true attention, and for the first time in her quest she hesitated. "This may strike you as being tawdry or mercenary, my lord, but I am an essentially practical person, and I suspect you value frankness highly enough to excuse any indelicacy of expression." *That's enough, Anne,* she told herself, and clamped her mouth shut.

He watched her for a while longer, then drew himself up, hands behind his back. The pose broadened his shoulders in a way that sent a quiet pulse through Anne's veins. The earl blushed only slightly and said: "Miss Pym, would you consider marrying me?"

Anne blinked. This she had not anticipated.

To give herself time to think about how to respond, she turned a critical eye upon the earl's person. Lord Underwood was only a few inches taller than she was. He was neither fat nor thin—he was simply solid, his body a set of straight up-and-down lines like a tree trunk that had access to an excellent tailor. He had a square face, held in place by a lumpy nose and weighed down by a stern chin. His eyes were dark and his hair plain brown, with a moustache that could just be termed elegant. He stood patiently beneath her examination and waited for her conclusions.

Physical charms aside, from his behavior after her cousin's seduction and marriage Anne knew that he had a steely sense of right and wrong and preferred to deal with problems in a head-on, forthright manner. This was someone she could lean on, yes—but he was also someone she could quarrel with if there came a need.

She came to a quick decision. "I would indeed consider marrying you, my lord," Anne said. "But I would also like to know why you should consider marrying me."

"Ah." Lord Underwood smiled and his shoulders relaxed. "Since my brother wed, I have been thinking it is time I started a family of my own. An earl needs an heir, and since John and Hecuba moved out, the house has had an empty rattle to it. I admire your character and the fact that you are moved to pursue what you want. It strikes me that this would be a fine quality in a wife—in a countess, especially—and in the mother of my children. More personally, I think we would suit well enough— and I don't feel particularly inclined to throw my heart upon the tender bosom of society. To parade myself before a host of strange and pale young misses, gouty fathers, and overeager mothers." Anne, whose mother could well be encompassed by the term *overeager*, grimaced in sympathy. The earl leaned forward, resting one hand on the desk. "Allow me to make my case to you. My fortune more than meets the requirements you listed, and three children strikes me as an excellent number to have. Your acquiring the title of countess would redeem your family's reputation at once, particularly since you and I would not have an initial scandal to overcome. In short," the earl concluded, "your problem and mine could be most speedily solved if we marry." He nodded, as though the gesture might convince her if his arguments had not.

His logic appeared sound, but... "Are you always this— efficient?" Anne asked.

"No," the earl admitted, mouth quirking. "Nor always so nonchalant. I can be a little irritable at times. I have my whimsical moods, the same as any man." He glanced away briefly, then brought those gray eyes back to meet hers. "But I feel very strongly that opportunities should be seized when they present themselves."

Anne nodded in approval. This was entirely in line with her own philosophy. She had always listened to her instincts, and they were speaking quite loudly at the moment. "I think we may do very well together, my lord," she said. "Would you care to call tomorrow at tea to propose formally? I can guarantee my father will be at home."

"It will be a pleasure, Miss Pym," said the earl, and held out a hand.

They shook, and the bargain was sealed.

ABOUT THE AUTHOR

Olivia Waite writes romance, fantasy, and science fiction, depending on the mood. She lives in Seattle.

In addition to her fiction, she reviews romances new and old in the monthly Kissing Books column for the Seattle Review of Books.

To get book updates, recommendations, fascinating research tidbits, and thoughtful longreads, sign up for her newsletter (tinyletter.com/OliviaWaite), which is sent out at the tasteful rate of every two months or so. You can also email Olivia at olivia.waite.books@gmail.com, or find her buzzing about on Twitter as @O_Waite

ALSO BY OLIVIA WAITE

Generous Fire

A buttoned-up schoolteacher, a smouldering headmaster, and a steam-powered vibrator.

Hearts and Harbingers

A charming Regency sex fairy tale.

Happily Ever Afterlives

Two Regency paranormals in one! First, a damned lord and an ambitious demoness fall in love in Hell; next, an incubus and a debutante waltz across a London ballroom.

"The Best Worst Holiday Party Ever"

My shortest, sweetest contemporary with a sommelier heroine and forensic accountant hero. Original mulled wine recipe included.